NYMPH

NYMPH

A Novel

Stephanie LaCava

VERSO
London • New York

First published by Verso 2025
© Stephanie LaCava 2025

All rights reserved

The manufacturer's authorized representative in the EU for product safety (GPSR)
is LOGOS EUROPE, 9 rue Nicolas Poussin, 17000, La Rochelle, France
contact@logoseurope.eu

The moral rights of the author have been asserted

1 3 5 7 9 10 8 6 4 2

Verso
UK: 6 Meard Street, London W1F 0EG
US: 207 East 32nd Street, New York, NY 10016
versobooks.com

Verso is the imprint of New Left Books

ISBN-13: 978-1-80429-991-3
ISBN-13: 978-1-80429-996-8 (US EBK)
ISBN-13: 978-1-80429-995-1 (UK EBK)

British Library Cataloguing in Publication Data
A catalogue record for this book is available from the British Library

Library of Congress Cataloging-in-Publication Data
A catalog record for this book is available from the Library of Congress

Typeset in Electra by Biblichor Ltd, Scotland
Printed and bound by CPI Group (UK) Ltd, Croydon, CR0 4YY

Nymph
A NOVEL

Stephanie LaCava

I never thought I would see more of an assassin than Michael Jordan ... until Kobe. Michael didn't care about anyone, but he had hobbies—golf, baseball. Kobe had no hobbies. His hobby was to assassinate you.

James Worthy

When my father was thirty, he lived on a ship somewhere in the North Sea with his brothers, Robert and Peter. That was after their father—my grandfather—summoned them and then left during the coldest month, just before his sons' arrival. He waited till they were on their way and then took himself off, disappeared from the North, showed up deep South. Return quiet; act like nothing happened. He would reclaim only one son in the end. To be fair to him, one was lost to another power; Robert became entangled in unsafe waters; gave up earthly control. My grandfather would cut the line on his second himself, when he fucked with family. A hard-conditioned clan is vigilant about legacy.

It was Robert's dealer who offered the three brothers a gig on a fishing boat. Robert had always been a low-key user, but when they hit the waters off Scotland, the addiction took a big hold. Nights on the boat were spent either playing cards below deck or working up top in yellow raincoats. There were ropes to pull, not unlike puppeteering. The ocean's no stage, though.

It was hard on Robert, my father told me. That was really all he ever said of him, a hardship circumscribed by this one story. Once things got really tough, in ways my father could weather more easily than his brother, Robert started to use more.

Sometimes he would disappear below for a few days and the captain—who really wasn't the captain, but a rich land-boy dealer who liked to play God—would seem extremely distressed. It was unclear why, as Robert did little to help on board. My father and Peter would cover for him. They were good at holding it down.

During one particularly bad storm, Robert reappeared and shared some of his stuff with Peter. My father abstained, which he claims was because of a large bird he'd seen earlier that day in the sky. He was like that with animals. Wild ones always appeared with a message. Perhaps that's why he named me as such.

Someone had gotten a kind of radio TV, and the two brothers had gone below to try to relax, possibly sleep. "Are you in your head?" Robert had asked my father when he refused to join them. Robert's favorite movie was *The Godfather*, and he was insisting that Peter watch it. "Fuck Pacino, to me that guy will always be *Panic in Needle Park*," my father once said when we walked past a poster at the movie theater.

Peter ODed that night. My father found him blue with bubbles around his mouth, next to a coil of rope and sea foam. The drugs had come from the captain. In truth, from the captain to Robert's hand to his brother's nose. Cold nose.

After that, my grandfather insisted my father and Robert come back to Boston, where he had landed. And they followed orders, because there was a body to be delivered, a funeral to have. Eleven months later, Robert received a call from the captain-dealer's girlfriend. They'd had a one-night stand way back when Robert had been fiending. He could tell the call was on speaker when she asked if he'd used protection. There was a male coughing in the background, the same hack he'd heard so many times on board. "No," he said. And she hung up.

She called back two days later and told him he had to take a test. The baby turned out to be his. The captain didn't care, raised him as his own. Named him Peter.

My father met my mother walking Long Wharf soon after.

The years that took me away from being a child would become the ones I'd cheated. When I was twelve, I decided I wanted to live in reverse. I think, though, this way of seeing was always there, like an inherited disease: to chase being unknown, not only by name but also by connections.

If you're signaled in utero that it's already too late, extra effort is required.

Welcome, you're cursed to stay a little longer.

In the Roman times, storytellers would introduce themselves by slipping in some talk of bloodlines to lend their story legitimacy. My father died three times before I was thirty.

Old noblemen flaunted their house, thinking criminals couldn't come from the same place as scholars. How wrong they were.

You're a fool, too, to think family connections let you skate past accusation. Nowadays breeding can signal the opposite of exoneration.

The withdrawn are the privileged few. None of our kind have time.

Some strange partnership my parents had, and it extended into the gloom of their professional lives. I knew very little about my father's and my mother's commitment—no clear facts until I turned eighteen. I was born with expert intuition; the expert marksmanship I had to work at.

Feelings can never change the contracted plan. Well, maybe in one instance, and even then it's more intuition and romance than plain feelings. A chance meeting and the clan may expand. Birth is non-negotiable. (If anyone can say they tried to get out of it, I can.) I would fight it, but the end is inevitable. You get a second chance to have the family you wanted, but it doesn't always arrive on time or in the form you expected.

When I asked my father why he didn't wear a wedding ring, he told me he didn't believe in that sort of contract. That we don't have contracts with our ancestors or our mothers, so why would we with our romantic partner? A dyad ride or die love was the top of the hierarchy, not that he believed in hierarchies.

No contracts between people regarding lived connections, no signatories save for the unseen. A bond is not always formed in extended time. It can happen in an instant, which was the way things happened to him, as they happen to many people in the world far away from safeties known.

Storytelling is a gift of facts contracted to fiction. I was named Bathory because a good cover is lore.

My father loved black metal, in particular a Swedish band called Bathory, which was the name of an old-world, forever-young female killer. I'd rather die than be directly named for such a woman without some remove. Bathory the band was not the same as Bathory the murderess. Frontman Thomas "Ace" Börje Forsberg, stage name Quorthon, knew the potential in linking metal music to the powerful Norse mythology in his performance. Lyrical in both senses.

My parents decided that Bath, pronounced "Bat," was the coolest diminutive. Quorthon, with his Scandinavian birthright, fire-breath, and pentagrams, loved Wagner and—not Satan, but Satan's story. Edgy, somehow apolitical. An understanding of how to sell things and not be the actual thing. How signifiers cancel themselves out.

Silencers.

And maybe it wasn't even that serious at not being serious. Maybe old Norsemen saw Odin coming down from the sky, as a force not of good or evil, but only a force. This is how I feel things. Some gods or demons commit crimes, others make mischief and mysteries. Punish those that cause pain. A crime can alleviate pain. Nymphs and angels.

I know my origin story; I had a feel of it before it was told to me. When my mother conceived me, she and my father were living in Oslo. Strange, sleepy place for two assassins; nothing much happens aboveground. But there is an underground. And legends of the forest, and higher up, in the air, more legends still. My father hated the cultural emphasis on everyone fitting in for the so-called collective good, and reckoned the place suffered for the modern lack of regard for those legends.

And so, my parents created a nest of their own ideals. What do you call a bat house? They lived not far from a body of water, which they privately called Asa Bay. My mother would go swimming every morning before doing anything else. There were seagulls and sea-found swans, with curious black heads. It was quiet, serene. And my parents remained committed to each other and in love, and committed to work that was not quiet or serene.

When my mother became pregnant, something changed. She found it harder to keep everything straight. My father said he'd always known she had a tendency toward this kind of messiness—some mistakenly call it darkness. It's never the evil kind, but the sort that doesn't let you see. Interior fog. You fumble in the dark.

Everything with my mother was intense, lived, and intentional. When she met my father, it was love at first sight. Everything in one moment. It's a strange myth that it takes time to know someone. You can both assume the worst of intentions at the outset and know the soul wager. The lack of days is a metric of your risk tolerance. I would learn later that love at first sight does take time, its veracity not always revealed in a linear model. My mother's life found immediate meaning in my father. Suddenly she didn't want to run headfirst into fire. She had been good at her work because, as she'd pass on to me, she was unafraid of death. Truly unafraid.

Meeting my father made her suddenly vulnerable; having a reason to want a future was something new. Living was easy how she had known it to be. Being pregnant gave her exponentially more reason to fight for her days, and this was terrifying. She became withdrawn, my father said. Not only from people, as she'd always been (a beautiful hermit, waiting to venture out only for work or when he was close), but also from her brave, crazy worldview. She no longer even wanted to go with him anywhere, at any time, to watch. I guess a part of him was inside her anyway.

My mother became what some would call depressed. As her belly grew, it only got worse. One day when my father went out to buy groceries, she tied stones to her legs and walked down to the water's edge. There was no one else in sight. She waded off the mossy shore and let go. In less than a minute, a fisherman who had been hidden by a tree dove in and pulled her up. Somehow, he was able to use his knife to cut the stones loose. He saved my mother, and he saved me. This is also why I think I'm named in a roundabout way after Norse mythology. No one ever saw the fisherman again. I'm not sure he ever existed.

"Bat-bat-bat-bat-bat!" The other children said my name over and over again even before any of us learned to talk. Without language, I was already girl-animal-weapon.

When I was small, my mother would take me walking in the nearby park. We were living in Boston at the time, Winter Hill. There was an elementary school with a map of the United States drawn on the uneven concrete of the playground. Nearby, three basketball hoops, one bent like a spoon, all without nets. On warmer mornings, I would sit and play along New England with Cookie, my stuffed donkey. He was always going on a journey, full of adventure and magic.

I would sit there for hours holding him by his mane, hand-hopping him from one chalk-outlined state to another, my mother watching from a bench across the court. She would sit back, arms crossed, sunglasses on, and never turn her head. She didn't look at her phone or bring a book. Never. Just sat there for what seemed like hours looking out, always dressed in the same outfit: a camel-colored sweater, white T-shirt, and black or gray men's pants. I thought for years that she stole my father's things but then realized that would have been impossible. He was six foot two and looked a little like a warrior. She was built like a ballerina, her slimness hidden by the baggy pants. Being hidden was important to her.

My mother had two pairs of shoes: black lace-up boots with low heels and gray old-man sneakers. Even though we went out so early it was still dark, she would wear sunglasses and a baseball cap. Sometimes I would ask to borrow the glasses. Before I could talk, I would reach for them. And she would pull away and refuse. I thought they were the reason she could always find animals I couldn't see. Her brown-red hair was sometimes pulled back or tucked under the baseball cap, which she kept in the closet at the front of our house. There were all sorts of hats inside, a disproportionate number for two adults. Nothing ever had corporate logos, only those of New York and Boston sports teams.

I later found out that these two factions were enemies, and the silhouette of entwined letters, a logo. The "Y" trapped inside the "N" became "New York," an example of the kind of sign other people were able to easily read. I knew the map of America like this too, could close my eyes and see each state, and then the larger shape. It was the section where Cookie played that was hard-logged, though I knew it would be meaningful one day. For now, I lived with my crazy parents there.

One morning, the darkness just starting to lift, I decided I would go to the sandbox. Cookie had stayed home with the flu, so I was looking for an imaginary bunny. I had no interest in building anything that could be instantly broken down, and figured it was the same for the other kids and that they would want to find a bunny, too. So, I ran through their castles of sand and almost-moats. They were angry and never forgot. And these kinds of things become more serious as they catch, like snowballs in the form of real live children already looking for scapegoats. I was only looking for bunnies.

There was a kind of omnipotence to both my parents, energetic, real-time. They were able to predict other people's moves and their needs. Perhaps this is why I didn't speak until later. I read first. Every book I could find: signs and letters. They were all easy to say aloud, but this didn't help decode the people around me. I would walk over the playground's swinging bridge holding tightly to the shaking chains. And I would hum to myself and watch as the other children stayed away.

These other children already knew how to talk, and they could talk about me and all I could do was assume that special form of mine as girl-animal-weapon, someone who couldn't be hurt because she wanted different things.

"Hey, you okay back there?" My father was looking at me in the rearview mirror. Green eyes hovering above a strange silver symbol swinging back and forth. My father's friend Tom was slouched low in the passenger seat wearing a fisherman's hat, sunglasses, and black hooded sweatshirt. "How far are we?" he asked my father, who waved him off. When he said "far" it sounded like "fah." The same thing happened when he said "car." My father slipped into this habit, as well, but only when he'd had too much to drink.

"I'm good, but Cookie needs some water."

"Who's Cookie?" asked Tom.

"It's her bunny," my father said sternly.

Tom visited every now and then. And when he came, my father always seemed a little on edge, which was rare. They had this way of interacting like they were of the same breed. I understood it best in animal terms. I once overheard Tom tell my father about a shop he ran somewhere in New York City, although he didn't look much like a shopkeeper to me.

"It's not a bunny, it's a donkey, Dad."

"It looks like a bunny to me. You love bunnies."

"This is a donkey, though. See its little pointy ears and long tail?" Cookie was my only stuffed animal. I didn't understand why other children required so many toys. One creature who had an intense interior life and liked to go on adventures was plenty. Like my parents were with each other, Cookie and I were a couple of a kind, a strange and inescapable pair. Despite my groans and protestations, I liked that no one could even tell what kind of animal he was, just as they couldn't tell what I was. Cookie and I could always move quietly, and we would.

"How much longer? Are we there yet?"

"We have a long time to go, Bath. Why don't we play a game?"

"The game!"

"What's that?" Tom asked. "Bro, can I put the radio on?" My father waved him off again.

"You just have to say the name of an animal."

"Lizard."

"Donkey." I saw my father's eyes become smaller as he smiled.

"Komodo dragon," Tom said.

"That's two," I said.

"It's one animal," my father confirmed.

"You lose," Tom said.

"It's not like the silent game."

My father's eyes were suddenly somewhere else. In the mirror I could see the bow of his lips lift slightly on the right. He saw me clocking this and course-corrected, met my gaze.

"Great White Shark."

"Spider-tailed horned viper."

"Son-of-a-bitch," I said, remembering what I had heard my father yell from way back in his office that morning.

"Bath!"

"What?" I knew even then that if you said the bad thing and took hold of it, somehow you could break away from assumed cause and effect.

"Hilarious," my father said, shooting me a stare and reaching his right hand back to tenderly hold my leg for a couple of moments. "A few years ago, when Bath first started to talk, we asked her one day, 'What's the magic word?'" He added, still holding me, "You know, like trying to teach her manners?"

"Right: 'Please,'" Tom said.

"No, that's the thing. You know what she said? 'Abracadabra.'"

"Bath, where are you? It's time for your bath!" my mother said, not realizing I was behind her. I started laughing.

"That's funny."

"I love you," she said. I had taken my dress off and laid it folded on the floor next to the tub. She started to loosen the braid on the left side of my head. I undid the little black ribbon at the base of the one on the right.

"Love you," I had trouble saying the "I." I was only six. I dropped the ribbon on the folded dress. We saved them every day to use again the next. I wondered how old I would be before we stopped the pigtails. They were an easy way of taming my very thick red-blond hair. When I was born, I was blond, which didn't make much sense. It was nowhere in the family bloodline. Scandinavian by proxy, by savior.

"It's just how you like it," my mother said, sitting on the edge of the bath, legs straight out in a V, finger testing the water.

"I can go in even when it's really hot or really cold." I looked in the mirror. The left side of my hair had come undone in gravity-resistant frizz. My mother smiled at me through the glass.

"You're a sea priestess."

"What's that?"

"It's a kind of half-good-witch-half-mermaid."

"Half sea beast, half girl?"

She nodded and got off the edge and sat on the tiled floor. I was watching my toes come up through the bubbles. I arched my neck back so that my hair would hit the water in a limp collapse. A thin-tentacled water creature. My mother started to sing something and I looked at her, the other side of my head falling wet, too, no trace left of those wayward airborne strands. When I raised my head, my hair was heavy where it had been weightless. "What are you singing?"

"It's an old song, one my mother used to sing to me."

"That's not English?"

"No, it's Latin."

"Will you teach me?" She nodded. "Not the song, Latin."

"Bath," she said, smiling like I'd never seen before.

"What?"

"You are something else." Her eyes were looking directly at mine, her mouth closed, cheeks up.

I didn't understand. "No," I said, "I'm a girl."

She fished out the bar of soap that had fallen in the tub and handed it to me. The same one my father used. I didn't have the language for the smell, but always thought "America," even though its name was Irish Spring. I knew you could buy it at the gas station and pharmacy, a green box with lucky clovers. "You need to wash behind your knees."

"Can I get my nails painted?"

"I think you need to wait until you're a little older."

"Some of the girls at school have glitter polish."

"I have a friend who can start teaching you Latin. We'll go see them on Thursday."

We had moved to a larger place in Somerville, past Cambridge, within three years of arriving in town. I had been told this was so that my father could set up a home office. But there had also been strange things happening around our apartment building. I had grown to love the place near the university, with its nearby sandbox and playground, big bathtub and dark windows you could see out of, but where no one could see in.

The move happened quickly. I was taken out by an every-now-and-then babysitter to places like the Isabella Stewart Gardner Museum to see different, miniature lands in paintings. A visit to little houses in lieu of a leave-taking of my own. No warning, I was privy to no plans, but my room was all set up when we arrived at a different address than the one we left from. I was most upset by the sudden move, because it meant the end of my in-person Latin lessons. It would be too far for my mother to take me back to campus. Still, two straight years of study at such a young age would prove handy for the course that had been set.

As soon as we got there, the sitter vanished, and I was told I was never allowed in the back part of the house. No questions entertained, which was strange, as they were otherwise encouraged. My parents then insisted on taking me to some cartoon movie. My father fell asleep in the theater. Afterwards we went for pizza at Ernesto's, a joint in a strip mall across the way. "E-nesto's" in big white script, hung up over an awning shared with the rest of the shops. It was that night that I told my parents I thought it was funny how in the movies you see the bad guys have families that they love. And then they smiled at one another and then at me and said, "Yes, that is funny."

The rule wasn't aired again but nor was it breached, and with this silent adherence my reverence for it grew: I simply couldn't walk over the silver line on the floor; it kept that one part of the house separate from all the other rooms we lived in. I was mostly fine with this, until I heard a girl in my class talk about her own father's office. How she would go visit him and they would order McDonald's! She said there were office supplies with the company logo, and that he was a trader. I thought this meant a fishmonger or traiteur, as in French fairy tales. Or perhaps even something worse, a betrayer. She explained that his office was a room inside another room. Not a marketplace, but somehow a market. There were computer screens and flashing digits. This same girl called me "stupid" and "retarded" when I wasn't able to answer her questions about my own father. All I knew was that every day he would get up and go right across that silver line to the back part of the house.

One morning, I woke with a fever. Babysitters or even visitors were rare by then, if they came at all. I knew my mother would cancel whatever plans she had to stay with me. "You should lie in bed for a little longer," she said, without turning around, knowing I had snuck downstairs. "Bath, come on. Do you need something?" I could see her at the sink, her sleeves rolled up past her elbows, safe from suds.

"No, it's okay. I will go back to bed." I turned to leave and then turned back again to see if she was watching. Her attention was on her phone now, I assumed to inform the school of my absence. I set off in the opposite direction of my bedroom, down the small corridor, over the metal transom to a chamber with a glass door. I couldn't see in, but within seconds it opened, my father's green eyes staring back at me.

"Bath, you know you're not allowed up here. Where's your mother?"

"I-I—"

"Why are you not at school?"

"I have a fever," I said, and fell dramatically to the floor. He laughed and shook his head. Then he bent down and put his hands under my arms to lift me upright. I could smell him. I was wearing a nightgown with a tiny pink rosette and thin white straps. He kept on holding me in the air as he kicked open the door. Two-tier creature: me, hair static-fixed to his T-shirt, legs L-shaped. Him: arms steadfast, in prison exercise form, lowering me to the ground. (I'd once walked in on him doing a particular suite of moves, which he explained as his workout from back when he was in jail once upon a time in some place with a name I can't now remember.)

My father smiled and sat down on the floor next to me, crisscrossing his legs like mine: shoulders back, chest forward, hands on knees. That crazy ability to keep his hands still, even in midair. I tried to take one and at first it went stiff, then his fingers relaxed over mine. Taking the great risk of running into his office had brought a great reward—I'd broken a hard rule, so something hard could be won. My father was good at making sure he met whoever he was with exactly where they wanted to be seen. "Are you okay sitting like that?" I asked.

"Yeah," he said. All six feet two inches contorted to stay close to his daughter. We sat there together on standard-issue flooring, like some kind of poster from the golden age of advertisements. The entire space of the room-inside-the-room was covered with wall-to-wall gray carpet. A connected space looked like a recording studio with its thick foam walls. In the main chamber were stacked rows of square screens, squat picture-boxes. "Why are you watching all these old fashion shows?"

"Old-fashioned shows?" He corrected me knowing well what I'd meant to say.

"Yes. And why is that one basketball?" The last box on the bottom right showed a stream of reels of a tall, handsome black man who looked familiar. In one clip, he was high-school age. White letters with shivered edges, flanked like cartoon racers bleeding horizontally top and bottom, crossed at the bottom of the image. Nothing read sharp or clear, unlike the strange monotone screens nearby.

Then the basketball star as a young man, looking already somehow old. I was still figuring out how to work it out, but I had a kind of ability to square someone's carriage with their internal state. By old, I didn't mean body-failing old, I meant on another plane, attached to the ground in 2D? 4D? My mother had promised to get me books on this when I went to talk to her about it. She had already known that it was there, in me.

This is why I decided to like basketball—and later, baseball—because it had rules and courts that weren't feudal. The commitment was to be the best in a tangible metric, to practice, to work. It was clear. And here was this man, a boy then, talking into the camera, and I could tell he was gonna be huge, and then he would die. I could feel it.

"He's dead. That's an old highlight-show thing," my father said. I nodded and we watched together in silence. The man looked at the camera with the bearing of someone who feels not only that they belong on earth, even as one among all us others, but that the earth belonged to them, even if it only would for a short while.

"Unfortunately, because of lack of communication with my peers, I wasn't often invited to parties or friendly gatherings of a weekend so on Fridays and Saturdays I would take myself and my basketball to the rec room and dribble myself to exhaustion," said the man in the movie.

I didn't know what a peer was. "A peer is someone who sees?" I asked my father.

He laughed. "Peer can mean 'to see, to look out.' But not when it's a person; it's not a lookout. It can mean someone at your level." He paused and shook his head. "In Kobe's case—that's the late Kobe Bryant, one of the greatest basketball players of all time—he just means kids that were in his class at school."

"They weren't at his level?"

"Everyone's at the same level, Bath. As in, all humanity, all of one kind. Look at us sitting here. Same sightline to the screens, each of us the same span from the other. But there are other levels, ones that aren't up and down or better-than, worse-than.

Ones that are complicated to compute or even see—" I stopped him with a wave of my hand.

"I understand," I said, and he believed me, when really I was scared. "Why are there so many of them?" I tried to shift the intensity. "The old-fashioned televisions?"

"I like them like this, but the wires are new. I had them adapted so now the cables pull information from all over the world and onto these modest screens. I prefer the old sturdy boxes." My father liked to wire things; I had noticed him doing this in my room behind the vanity. One day he was in there, and the next there was some kind of device attached to black lines coming from my wall. No explanation. The car was also wired, but in a different way. It still had the old-school cassette player, which pleased my mother, but there was also satellite radio. She liked to listen to Radio 4, to the shipping forecast. She said it soothed her.

"They connect to all over the world?"

"Yes, these right here are getting signals live from places you can't even imagine."

"Like where?"

"Like all the way on the other side where it is nighttime."

"Nighttime?"

"And other things."

"Other things?" There was a sudden buzzing, and one of the screens started to show people fighting: figures running and then combat and firestorm. "Is that real?"

"Yeah," he said.

"Why don't you do something?"

"What do you mean?"

"You are seeing it here, because you can help?"

He paused and opened his mouth a little, held my knee. "I am seeing it here, so I can't help."

"What do you mean?"

"If I were there I could do something, but I'm here." It was very confusing the way he explained it. His non-answers always reworked my questions in their own strange way.

"And why the basketball man?"

"Ah, that screen is something different than the others. It's a channel: ESPN. Sports. Sometimes there are shows that talk about legendary athletes, but only the best ones."

"ESP?"

"ESPN. That I don't ever watch live, only the shows where they present things that have already happened."

"What?"

"Some people like to watch sports games live as a hobby. It's not for me." He gestured around at the screens. "These, though. Higher stakes, real time, bigger arena. Only I usually know who will win."

"How?"

"Well, I guess that's not always true."

"Why?"

"Because algorithms don't account for magic."

"I'm hungry."

"You should go." His hands had gone solid, eyes fixed to the top screen. "Go to your mother."

"Can't you come and help me?"

"I have to finish here."

"You never finish here."

"I have to do a little work on my own. Now go."

"Can they see us?" I asked.

"Who?"

"The screens? The other side?"

"The screens, no. The other side: Yes, I'm certain."

I pulled up the hem of my nightgown and stepped over the line that separated the office from the main hall.

A little after that day in my father's office, I asked if he would buy me some of the jerseys like the man in the video wore. I wanted to keep it with me, that not-even-an-hour on the floor together. The calm exchange quickly broken by an outside explosion. Not a real one, not that time, at least. Kobe still on the screen talking in perpetuity. Aeternum.

That's how you live forever. The signal on the ancient TV screens, static all, until the fuzziness reassembled itself as your picture, your image. They will blow you up. But if you're not known, they can't even put you back together. They are not your peers, but instead a kind of police team in the sky. Cameras to unbound angels and demons. Nobody knows for sure who's going to fall.

The basketball jersey was to figure for me like the lockets other girls got from their fathers. You can't wear the picture of someone who can't be seen. I wanted to feel close to him, his peace and smell. Smell and peace. That cheap soap and smoke and those outsize ideals, or the lack of them, which is the same in a way.

My father told me to ask my mother. She preferred me to wear jeans or corduroys and button-downs with Peter Pan collars. I told her I'd wear the jersey over a long-sleeved shirt with a skirt and knee socks, a look I'd refused otherwise. Maroon mesh with white stripes: Kobe's high school team, Merion. She eventually gave in, because of her guilt at having thrown me into a new class right at the end of the school year. All things were considered, except the consideration of what could disrupt my short little life.

One day she came home, her bag filled with new things. She handed me the clothing straight away, pulling the tags off as she passed it over, but told me that I'd have to wait a little while for the other purchases. I could see through the bag that they were stacked and rectangular, like books. Five or six of them, seven maybe.

I ran upstairs to try on the jersey and stand in front of the mirror on my vanity. That strange piece of furniture protruding into the center of my bedroom had traveled with us everywhere it could be carted. It was the only thing, object or person, parents aside, that was a steady presence in my life. An antique with a huge round mirror in between its two wooden wings, it had a strangely perfect hole in the right-hand side of its upper demilune, a puncture surrounded by a web of fissures, straight through past the wooden back. I know because once I stood on my desk chair and put my finger in there. The rest of the glass was unmarked. Of course, the black wire thing on the wall behind it was new. I couldn't understand why my mother always insisted on keeping the vanity.

I pulled the jersey on over my clothes. The Peter Pan collar came out on top to rest over the maroon-and-white ticking. I looked like a medieval page boy—white collar slivers over mesh vest. I didn't like it and so tore it all off to try on the shirt alone.

This time as a dress, hem to my knee. I put my right hand on my hip. It was so big. I remembered that there was a belt that had been packed among my things. I ran to see if I could find it in the closet.

The tiny brown leather whip was curled high up on the shelf, resting on the second set of bed sheets. I could see the metal clasp catching the light. It would have been easy to call my mother, easier to ask my father, who could reach anything at any height. But I wanted to do it myself. And so, I took the funny wood and metal chair I used for reading and homework and carried it to the closet. Splinters from the seat back caught in the holes of the mesh jersey. I peeled the two apart and placed the chair facing the back corner of the closet. Even when I stood on top of it, I wasn't quite high enough to grab the belt. I seized one of the wire hangers that dangled just below my chest, and angling its hook upwards I caught the belt's gold closure and pulled it down, stepping neatly off the chair at the same time. Standing in front of the mirror, I fastened the belt around my waist. It fit.

"Bath!" My mother startled me.

"Oh my God, what?"

"Why are you climbing on chairs?" She stood in the doorway where it would have been impossible for her to see inside the closet. Her face broke into a smile. "Look at you. That's good." She walked over and hugged me close.

"How did you know I was climbing in the closet?" I asked.

I wore the maroon jersey dress to my new school the following week, and that annoying blond girl called me stupid.

"Girls don't wear those kind of shirts," she snarled, her face so close to mine that I had to step backward into the painted brick wall. There were two other children with her, another girl in our year and an older boy. I looked over his right shoulder, because I knew he wanted me to look at him. My only friend, a classmate named Alyssa who lived across the street, was out sick that day.

"Why can't you do normal things, like play with the other girls," he spat at me. "Why aren't you saying anything?" I looked him in the eye then, and his hands flew up wild in the air. "Why are you staring at me like that?" He tensed and his left hand came up overhead. Some kind of shiver-energy ran from his eyes to his hand and back, invisible strings that couldn't hold. I saw it coming and I didn't move. He slapped me, hard, across the left cheek. I knew he would do it. I didn't care. The strange thing was that he started to cry almost as soon as his hand connected.

We were both taken to the principal's office. Almost no one believed that I had done nothing to provoke him. The female teachers were the most skeptical. Principal Williams, a tall, calm man who wore old basketball shoes with dress pants, seemed to believe me. He kept nodding his head and grinning without teeth. None of the others would look at me, only at the boy and each other, conspirators before I told my side of the story. Out of nowhere, the playground attendant, a lady named Danvers, started yelling at me. "You should go home and get changed. Pants are required as part of our school's dress code." It was only late in this skewed and silly judicial system that anyone thought to add that to the warrant. "Principal Williams, she clearly provoked him. He's a good kid, I've never seen him—"

The principal started to speak, then stopped, came around behind me and put his hands on my shoulders. He kept them there, as Danvers glared at me sidelong. "Okay, Miss Danvers, why don't you leave her with us and go back to the playground," he said.

Only after she was out of sight did he lift his hands off of me.

My father had to pick me up, because my mother hadn't answered her phone. They always call the mothers first. My father didn't say a word until we got in the car. He started the engine and let the car idle, as if to be sure no one outside the car could hear, though no one was near enough to anyway. Besides, the radio had come on, reciting the wind forecast, visibility and barometric pressure for Peterhead.

"The way people behave, it's never really about you. It doesn't change who you are."

There was a knock on my bedroom door. "Who is it?" I asked, knowing it was her. My mother walked in, carrying a parcel wrapped in tan paper tied with white string. "I have a gift for you."

"Why?" I was sitting on my bed still wearing the jersey dress that had caused all the drama at school.

"I got them for you the other day." I was waiting for her to bring up what happened, but she didn't. She handed me the package and came to sit next to me. "Wait to open it, just a moment, because I want to explain a little. They are a few books that my mother gave to me when I was your age. You will see that the author doesn't go by her real name. It's a name she made up. Kind of like us. Her family had a saying, 'Deo, non Fortuna'—"

"God, not fate," I interrupted her, translating.

"Yeah." She wasn't very impressed. "The writer took this and made her name out of it. This isn't to say she believed in it, maybe quite the opposite, but it was the root of a new fake identity. A lot of the books are . . . stories, but in the stories are lessons about living things."

"Why do you say it like that? Living things?"

"I don't mean not dead, but animated." I put the package on the floor next to my bed. "Fuck." I slipped up and said it aloud, and was annoyed at myself.

"Bath!"

"Sorry, I am getting the hiccups." My mother smiled. And that's how it first occurred to me that the Latin for "here," also meaning "now," was the same as for "then": hic. I was hiccupping nonstop, and my mother decided we should get some air. I changed into jeans and a T-shirt before following her into the kitchen.

"Drink an odd number of sips of water with barely a pause," she said, handing me a plastic cup. I followed her orders.

"It worked," I said without tremor.

"Always does."

"How do you learn things like that?"

"That's a good question. They come to you as you go."

"I can't do it anymore."

"What?" She stopped and looked at me.

"I can't go to school."

"Why?"

"It's so fucking boring." She nodded and put on her baseball hat, but took off her sunglasses, leaving them on the silver part of the stove. "It really is, and I don't have any friends except for Alyssa."

"One is all you need. You have us."

"That's such a mother thing to say."

She laughed. "I like Alyssa, we should all go out to eat together."

"Can't I have her over?" My mother paused and cocked her head. "Let's go to a movie together first."

"Can I just not go to school?"

"You have to go to school, at least till the end of the year. Think of it as a game where you know all the answers."

"I do, though."

"I'm proud of you. I think the problem is that they sense you don't really care if they accept you."

"Who is 'they'?"

"Your peers."

"They are not my peers." My father laughed as he walked into my room. "What are you doing here?" I said in an accusatory tone.

"I forgot something in the office. You guys were being loud."

"Mom got me a bunch of books." I gestured at the unopened package. "What did you forget?" I asked.

"Nice shirt," my father said, ignoring the question. I was wearing one of his old ones, inside out, from some band called Obituary. The cotton was super soft. My mother had asked me not to wear it to school with the silk-screened graphic on view. I didn't really ask or care why. She never wanted me to wear anything with an image or symbol, Kobe's jersey being the exception, and that didn't have a logo, only letters and numbers.

Some girls had their name embroidered on their jackets. Mine was already on the band's T-shirts, but those had always been forbidden. My mother wasn't fond of names on garments generally, and said that she'd heard other parents back in Boston say the same thing. It was a terrible idea to have children's names on their clothes, because anyone could pretend to know them. She always told me that if anyone ever called my name, I was to ignore them. We had hardcore "Don't Talk to Strangers" regulations.

Having "Bryant" on my back was a kind of coup, though one that had gotten me into trouble. "What did you forget?" I asked again.

"My gun," he said flippantly. I laughed.

"Haha, very funny." He nodded.

"Go put your shoes on. It looks like your mother wants to go do something. The gift will be a surprise for later." He paused and then gestured toward a book. "That's mine. How did you get that?" It was a book on the global history of paper money that I'd stolen from his stuff.

"Oh—I took that." I got up to find my indoor soccer shoes, knowing I had kicked one across the room earlier. It had landed between two stacks of books. I liked to keep all my books on the floor near my bed. I put the package from my mother on top on the stolen money book.

My father put his arm around my mother and she looked calm and happy. He whispered something in her ear, which I was sure had to do with me having meant to hijack the book. She turned her baseball hat backward and he kissed her good-bye before he walked out. I put on my shoes and pulled a black sweatshirt from the armoire next to the vanity.

"We need to get you some bookshelves," my mother said, standing in the doorway.

"I don't want bookshelves. I like them this way." She looked into the hall, first to the left, then the right.

"Now that your father's gone—open it." I followed orders again and went to pick the package off the floor.

The Demon Lover/ The Sea Priestess/ Moon Magic/ The Secrets of Dr. Taverner.

"All I can say is this is a way to teach you about magic things. And that a good story shows its middle to have not been the end, but that happens only at the end."

"What kind of cryptic nonsense is that?" I asked.

"Like a psyop," my father said from the hall, passing by the door again.

"Please." My mother shook her head and smiled. "I thought he was gone," she said to me quietly, leaning forward.

"What's a psyop?" I asked.

"Never mind. We need to go," my mother said.

"Where are we going?"

"I think we should take the car for a drive."

"Can I drive?"

"That's a few years away yet."

"Fine." I followed her down the stairs and out to the driveway. My parents shared an old stick-shift Jeep, which meant my father hadn't actually ended up leaving the house again. They were adamant that they only needed one car, one house, one child, one each of whatever sort of things that other people collected but could never use all at once. We both got in without saying anything. As soon as I shut the door, my mother pushed the see-through cassette deeper into the tape player and started the car. "Wagner," I said. She turned it off so we could speak. I took off my shoes and put my feet on the dashboard. "We have science class now. On Thursdays. Biology. The ocean."

"The silent, inward tides that govern men—These are my secret, these belong to me. Out of my hands he takes his destiny. Touch of my hands confers polarity."

"What?"

"It's in one of those books. Did you talk about the tides?"

"Yeah, and the layers, both above and under the sea. Sunlight Zone. Twilight Zone. Midnight Zone—"

"I want to take you to the seaside. Shall we go?"

"Right now?"

"We could go to a lake, but perhaps we'll take a trip somewhere later."

"It's almost spring break."

"We could go to Cape Cod."

"That's by the sea?"

"Yes, and not far. We could go see your grandparents' house. It's on the beach." My mother had never mentioned this before. Funny to say it that way, their house. She didn't like to be out in the sun, but I knew she liked to go to the beach at night with my father.

"I know all the oceans," I said.

"I've been to every one."

"Really?"

"Yes."

"Even the Arctic and Southern Ocean?"

"Yes. Ask your father about the North Sea when you discuss the other thing."

"Which thing?"

"PSYOP. The North Sea and psychological operations. There is a magnetism to that part of the world. I still think about it. All the time."

"That's what magnetism is," I said.

"Wow, Bath. Sometimes I forget how old you are."

"Real magnetism, like in the ground?"

"Yes, but also energetic."

"You're pulled there?" I asked.

"Exactly." She laughed and the radio came on, that strange stream of warnings of gales, numbers and directions.

"How do you know what you feel?" I had meant which one: the magnetic earth or the tides. The inner feeling or the physical sensation? But the first was also the second; the second created the first.

"You don't always. You will be off sometimes. The signals will come in and you will know they are signals but not always how to translate them. I can tell you this: if someone makes you feel confused, keep your distance. When it's unclear, it's clear. And when it's unclear, forgive yourself."

"Forgive myself?"

"For not knowing immediately. Be patient."

"But I always feel like I don't have time."

"I know."

"There was something the biology teacher said the other day that I didn't understand."

"Tell me."

"Every organism seeks safety."

"I don't know if that's true."

"Of animals or humans?"

"There's a difference between staying alive and trying not to kill yourself." As she turned the wheel, the lake came into view. "Look, let's get out and have a walk!" I took my feet off the dashboard and put my shoes back on. "Don't think too much, Bath. You'll take a new form soon."

39

It was strange to sit in the back, as I had when I was younger, but the fax machine thing—whatever it was—had to sit in the front seat on the passenger side. There was an uncanny feeling in being there behind my father, strapped into my seat, my knees pushed up to my chin. I remember watching his eyes in the rearview mirror, a short, rectangular movie every ride, to see if I could see anything in them. I don't think he realized I played this game, though he would catch me watching on occasion. Then the corners of his eyes would rise, and fall again as he kept them on the road, but somehow on the periphery too. Always alert himself, he was unbothered by hypervigilance. Being always alert, and always being beside someone who was always alert must make safety feel strange, which doesn't entirely account for my parents' love, but does for so much else.

My father liked to keep the driver's side pushed far back. And I had chosen to sit on that side, where my car seat had always been as a child. The left side, except when we went to the British Isles and all that. I liked the familiar feeling of resting my hand on the ledge below the plastic putty handle. It was an old model for the time, and there was a silver peg you could push down to lock the door that popped up like a mole from its hole when you unlocked it.

"You okay back there, Bath?"

"I'm fine."

"You're gonna like one of these guys, if I know you. He's really cool."

"One of your friends?"

"The son of—he's older than you, but not by so, so much."

"How do you know these people?"

"I've known them all for years, but this one is the youngest by a stretch. The only other kid besides you, and now he's . . . well, he's not a kid these days. They all met you many times when you were small, though I'm not sure you'd recognize them. I'm not sure if you'd have seen their faces properly, to be fair."

"Why wouldn't I have seen their faces?"

He waved his hand. "They like to wear sunglasses all the time."

A large house was slowly coming into view down the way, cottage-like in shape but on a castle-like scale. In front were rings of stones and wild grass. My father pulled in and parked the car. He came around to get me out of the back before dealing with the equipment.

"Thank you, Daddy."

"You're very welcome." I stood up and shook out my shoulders. There were five other cars in the driveway. Three big SUVS and two 1980s-style coupes. "Check that Hammer," my father said, surveying the cars.

"Quite the party," I said.

"How did it feel to be back there? Been a while since you weren't in the driver's seat."

"It was nostalgic. I remember the smell too. Your smell. I can't believe you still smoke those things. I won't tell Mom."

"I don't do it in the house."

I nodded. "Do you need help with that?"

"No, no. It's fine. It's not so heavy." Just as soon he had opened the side door and bent over, a man appeared in front of us. He looked like he hadn't slept in days and smelled like the back of the car five times over.

"Hi," he said, looking at his palms and wiping them on his black corduroy pants; his white T-shirt was covered in grease stains. It took him a moment to notice me, but when he did the noticing was obvious. "You brought someone?"

"Yes, she's cleared."

"Oh yeah? She looks all of fifteen."

"I know how to drive."

"Okay. What's your name?"

"Bathory."

"What? Like the black metal band?"

"Yes." I could see my father smile.

"Will," his friend said, and my father shrugged. He motioned someone to come help. "This is Iggy, John's son."

"I know Iggy," my father said. I looked up and felt something I didn't have the language for. Iggy was half man, half boy, with eyes as steady as my father's but a gait that was ever so slightly off, and shoulders slumped forward. He pretended not to see me, or at very least refused to meet my eyes.

"Will, it's so good to see you," Iggy said to my dad, still making as if I wasn't there.

"You remember Bath?" my father said, gesturing to me. I smiled at him, head down, eyes up.

"I do." He had seen me. "She's grown up." His eyes made the bold move to my feet. I stuck out my hand. He looked at me. I pulled my hand back and acted shy. His look stayed on me a little too long, and then he ducked toward the car.

"Iggy, get that last thing," my father said. Iggy stuck his right hand up in the air and waved a "yes." My father stepped aside to let him angle into the car and lift out the metal machine.

"Follow me," Iggy said. My father and I fell into step behind him as he carried the piece of equipment almost like you would a tuba. He walked with a certain awkwardness; he was very tall, but it was as if with every other step he sunk a little into the ground. Solid there, and again over there, but then a soft give. Whatever his gait, nothing loosened his hold on the thing he was carrying. "Heads up, the whole crew is in there," he said. "Apart from Winston; he left earlier to go to town and get more food."

"I'm not worried. Bath here will be fine, she's used to this kind of thing." Iggy paused as if about to say something and then continued on in silence. There was classical music playing inside; I recognized it as we came closer. Iggy looked back at me after putting the machine on the long, rough wooden table in the entryway. I didn't know what to say or where to look, so I pretended to be trying to divine where the music was coming from.

There were what looked like very significant artworks hanging throughout the hall. One was a large sailing ship, its mast rendered as a cross. A smaller boat of little men appeared to sit calmly in the nearby murky waters. *"Christ in the Storm on the Sea of Galilee,"* Iggy said to me, flicking his chin at the painting. *"Study for the Programme,"* he continued as we passed a pair of dancing feet and the bow of a cello done in charcoal. "Rembrandt, Degas."

This was a strange place for a mansion outside of Boston. The interior was sparse; the room at the back was covered in wood panels as far as I could see. Metal chains held up the artworks, as if suspended from a clip in the back. The music seemed to be rising from somewhere below. A chant started. Someone came up next to me.

"Are you okay?" Iggy asked.

"I think so," I said. "Where's my dad?"

"He went to talk to someone, told me to find you and ask if you wanted something to eat. Would you like a hamburger or a hotdog?"

"We're barbecuing?"

"That's the plan."

"I don't eat meat," I said, shrugging.

"Oh. Well, can I get you a drink?"

"Yes, a whiskey," I said.

"What kind?"

"I was joking."

"Oh." Iggy was treating me like I was the same as him. Horizontal on his sight line, not female and not younger or any of the things that I was afraid would draw hurt to me.

The music ceded to a bass that hadn't existed before. Then the sound became something else, heavy metal hitting glass, no longer a composition on a page. Something shattered and fell, beat after beat onto something that didn't give. It took me a moment to realize this wasn't the music anymore. I started to hear the same sounds again, only sped up, the tempo awry and alarming, and I saw Iggy's coolness break. He was in front of me suddenly, arms out like a human shield. "Stay still," he said, but

I couldn't even imagine treating his words as something I should listen to. Instead, I ran out from behind him towards the noise. Something heavy and hard came at me from the left.

I opened my eyes as I recovered my breath and saw three men staring down at me. None of them looked familiar, and there was no sign of my father or Iggy. I knew enough not to say anything. I closed my eyes quickly, hoping perhaps I could pretend to be dead. One laughed, "We know you're in there." So I opened my eyes as wide as I could and tried not to blink, in defiance.

"There wasn't supposed to be any women here, never mind a child."

"I'm not a child," I said, sounding unafraid because I wasn't afraid. My whole childhood had been leading up to this. Of this I was somehow certain.

"Okay, then," he said back at me. "What do you think we should do?" He was dressed in assorted shades of faded black, unplanned and haphazard. The other two were outfitted much the same, but with padded vests. I imagined to myself that they were like the numbered bibs one would wear in a marathon race, and still I wasn't at all afraid. It took a moment before I realized my pants and shirt had been removed and I was crouched there in the corner wearing only my white underwear ruched all around the edges in lazy ruffles. There was some blood in the grain of the fabric, so I crossed my legs. "Are you hungry?" I asked.

All three laughed, out of discomfort more than mockery. "Hungry?" The one without a vest repeated.

"Yeah. I can make us some sandwiches."

"No," he said, and smirked at the others. "Do you have any other questions?"

"No." I said, crossing my arms over my bare chest, tilting my face downwards and looking up at them, showing the bottom whites of my eyes. The one without the vest stepped back and put his arm out so that one of the others could lunge forward at me. He stopped short. I could tell I had gotten to him and he couldn't stop his embarrassment from showing, even in front of the others. He looked physically uncomfortable, despite all his tactical gear and, I assumed, years of experience.

One of the men kicked my clothes back at me. I didn't move.

"Put your clothes on," he said. "And then leave. I don't ever want to see you again."

"Bath!" Iggy was waving to me from one of the rocks down the beach, where the breadth of the sand was smaller than any I had seen stateside. He was standing on a large lump of what was once lava, its perforations still showing despite the beatdown of centuries. I decided to take his wave as a kind of surrender, a submission. I had picked out my two-piece swimsuit weeks ago. Navy blue. I wasn't sure if I should take off my sandals or not. The flat leather soles would go slick with a little water; I could climb better without them. Or leave them on and crawl like a little creature, attached to the rocks. Iggy called, "Wait there!"

He buttoned up his shirt as he came closer. We looked at each other and he pushed his hair behind his ears. Eyes down again, he surveyed the landscape always changing before his feet. When he raised his eyes to see if I was still there, his brown hair fell in front of them once more. I smiled, but tried as hard as I could to keep all of the rest of me from moving, to keep myself from shaking. It was so hot that it was difficult to stand still on the sand; my now bare feet moved of their own accord to find a cooler spot, but didn't.

"Hello," I said, looking past him at the darker part of the sea. It was far too hot for his long sleeves.

"You just arrived?"

"About an hour ago. My father kept telling me he had to show me something and not to let him forget when we were on the plane. Turns out, it was two pieces of artwork in your castle. And then I had to listen to your father talk about them."

"It's far from a castle." He laughed. "I think you saw them already, in the house outside Boston." His face fell, as if he shouldn't have mentioned the setting from that night.

I laughed and pretended it didn't matter. "Oh, right, the Rembrandt." He smiled and shrugged.

"Good thing you escaped from the castle then. How did you find me? Do you want to walk to the village? I can't swim right now." The questions and statements fell out of him.

"Oh, sure—I have some clothes back in my basket."

"Basket?"

"I found this straw bag in the bathroom."

"Oh. That's not a . . . purse, but cute." I wanted to ask what it was. He seemed to quietly know everything, while what I knew was not very practical. You learn street smarts as a child through necessity, but I came to understand that I'd been reverse-insulated, until things got out of control. I had always known that I would have to learn scarier things once I reached a certain age. "There's an herb garden at the back house on the property that you might like. How did you know I was here?"

It was odd that he asked twice. I shrugged, although truthfully I had seen him, far away and small, from the window of the car when we drove up. He was unmistakable for many reasons.

"Your mother didn't know where you were," I said.

"That's not my mother." He appeared to get cold and walked ahead of me, then stopped and turned back to take my hand.

"Come, let's go to the crag."

"The crag?"

"Yes, a little cave-grotto. Give me that basket-purse." He let go of my hand and took the bag. He kept looking at me strangely, not in a way that was cruel or dismissive, but his focus put the fear of that into me. I was usually good at reading signals, but he made the usual signals make less sense. Was it he who was off, or me, or the combination we made? Was he miswired or did his wiring interfere with mine particularly? No matter, he now held the basket, and it was my turn for surrender. I had lost my grip on all my tricks. "Are you hungry?"

"Yes." With most people I subsumed my needs, but with him I felt I should amplify them—that he wanted to fulfill an ask, was looking for asks. Here we were, together again after the party day, but circling each other like two people meeting for the first time—no, not a new person, he never felt new, but like a fateful encounter between two kindred species.

I had read about this in one of my books. That you could know a psychic link with someone to be true, a chime waiting to sound in you both from birth. But then came all the unseen events that happen every day that follows the first—all the happenings that tip the scale toward action or passivity, and one can never know the weighting, not at first.

Did I know my own? Who's to say you ever know even yourself? This is what I wanted to talk to Dr. K. about. My mother was always saying I should start talking to her analyst. All I had here with Iggy was my teenage wits, and they were impure, too.

Not through my behavior, but because of someone else's even before I was born, and then again years after.

"I can take you to town after we look at the cave—or we can go before and get ourselves some provisions. You did good with the basket." I nodded. He was watching me as if he had never met a human being before.

"Is it far?"

"Oh no, but it's a tricky path. I know it well, though. I've been coming here since I was a little boy. My mother showed me."

We were walking single file on the rocks. He offered me his hand from behind as we both stepped onto a ledge in front of a dark opening. One step the other way and it was a straight fall to the ocean. He ducked inside, and I followed.

Iggy lit a match, which he seemed to have taken from nowhere. Amateur metal scaffolding showed against the back wall; an old, worn rug was spread at the back. "Oh my God. This is insane."

"I prefer it here to the beach."

I wanted to ask questions but stayed quiet. "Come, sit," he said, and sat down on the rug. I sat beside him. "Are you cold?" He didn't wait for an answer, just reached into my bag to pull out the yellow sweater. I took it from him and put it on. There was some kind of marking, a scar or a tattoo on the edge of his wrist. I saw it only for a moment before he covered that hand in a way that seemed natural but also aware. We sat together in silence, cross-legged in the stale cave. "What are those things around your ankles?"

"Bracelets, I like them." He nodded. "Why black and not gold?"

I wasn't sure if I should tell him the real reason. "I like them." He laughed. "You are funny." I shook my head. He laughed again. "Okay, I see. I haven't seen you since that day at the house." His mention of the attack felt both delusional and confident. It didn't matter what had happened, it was a day that was done. And we'd both survived to be here on this day. I wanted to be able to talk like that. He made me feel safe by proxy. Even so, he also felt more dangerous than anything I'd encountered before. "How do you like Boston?"

"It's fine, although I don't want to stay there. It's not exactly Boston; we moved from there."

"Where do you want to go?"

"I don't know."

"That's okay, you don't have to know. I didn't know till I got there, that I didn't want to be at school."

"College? Why?" I couldn't help myself.

"It's not for me. I'm not a professional—not like that." I nodded. "I may come by Boston soon. We should hang out." I didn't understand why he would want to see me. I couldn't even carry on a normal conversation. "Your father tells me you like to read, something like book a day?"

"Yes." He seemed to think my reticence was charming, a challenge, or both.

"What are you reading now?"

"I brought a few books with me."

"I hope you brought enough, because you will have trouble finding English books around here."

"I read Latin too."

He started to laugh and then stopped himself. "Okay, let's go to the village. Enough of this. You've seen what there is." He said it like his home had been a disappointment. "Do you like ice cream?"

"I love ice cream."

"Good." I took off my sweater. I had been roasting for ten minutes. Iggy was focused and quiet, carrying the basket in the crook of his arm. I tied the sleeves around my body. Over one shoulder, under the opposite shoulder, diagonal across my chest. It pushed in on the bikini string that was held between its two pieces of navy fabric.

"It's only a few more minutes." We walked side by side for another half hour before coming to the top of the hill. The road to the town was unpaved and flat.

"You never told me what books you brought."

"One is called *The Golden Ass*. I have a pair."

"In English and Latin?"

"How did you know?

"I know."

"I can appreciate that." He smiled and looked down.

"The man who runs the shop where we can get ice cream is really cool. I've known him for years. We have an understanding. When I was little, he used to point his chin to the freezer case and I would steal one of those chocolate Magnum bars. Once a week, all summer long, for over a decade."

"That's so sweet."

"It made me feel special, that I had my own secret from my parents. What's funny is my father taught me how to steal food from the fancy grocery store. He called it shoplifting. No one says that anymore, hmm? He said it was okay to do at certain fancy places. The ice cream shop, as you're soon to see, is the exact opposite. I was warned about cop trouble elsewhere."

We turned a corner to see a stone wall that started small and then grew up. A few more minutes and we couldn't see over it. We turned right again and there was an old building with a bent metal sign and one freezer case. "This is it."

"Super charming."

"I want you to meet Freddie." Iggy took my hand and led me through the large stone-lined entryway. The shelves held only a handful of essentials, cans of food, a few large bottles of water and some plastic containers of candy. He looked suddenly upset, an expression I'd never seen on him before. He fiddled with his sleeve, but when he saw that I was paying attention he stopped.

"What's wrong?"

"I've never come in and not seen Freddie's hat or newspapers." A pretty young woman wearing a tan apron and maroon sundress came out through a curtain hanging in the back.

"Where's Farhoud?" Iggy asked calmly in a language I couldn't place. His gesture confirmed my amateur translation. She put her lips inward, looked at me and said something. Iggy took his wallet out and tried to angle so that I couldn't see his hands. But I knew the color and pattern of the bills. He laid the equivalent of $5,000 on the counter.

The woman's hand flew on top of Iggy's before he could take it back down. And I saw a scar show out of Iggy's cuff, tissue the same color as the border of the red printed currency. "Why?" she seemed to be saying, walking behind the faulty counter, keeping her hand over his. Her eyes translated for me. Iggy said something very simple, then walked out. I followed. He paused to look through the ice-crusted top of the freezer case. There were rows of coated-paper sealed ice cream bars, a few vertical, to save space.

We walked together in silence back toward the cave. I tried to be calm and not question him. The landscape turned from beach to pop as we passed a flat field of yellow flowers. I'd seen these before in France, expanses of mustard or lavender that ended suddenly. You could smell the change. Also the shift in Iggy.

"Can I do anything for you?" He stopped short at this.

"What do you mean?"

"Can I do anything for you?" I repeated, too paralyzed to do anything else.

He shook his head. "I'm sorry. I promised you ice cream—I . . ."

"I'm not a child!"

"Right." He refused to look at me the way he had earlier. I wanted his old look back.

"That woman at the shop wasn't much older than me."

"That's exactly it, in two senses."

"What do you mean?"

"Let's go back to the house. I promised Admiral Will I wouldn't keep you for too long."

"Why do you call my father that? What did you pay her for?"

"A decade of stolen ice creams."

My father had been in the back of the taxi, with me and my mother in the front seat, when we saw the signs. We were on our way home, back from France. I'd been going through my phone, looking at pictures from the vacation. Peering over my shoulder, my father had stopped my swiping at the one with Iggy sitting on the floor playing cards. It was taken in the living room, in front of the masterpiece by the fireplace. "I can't believe that's not real," he said, zooming in with his fingers. My mother inhaled sharply in what I thought to be out-of-character commentary on his disclosure. Then, I looked up.

The front door was fractured, what was left held together as a kind of star.

"Fuck," my father said.

"Will, please."

"What happened?"

"Sir, can you take them back to town?" my father said.

"Why?" I asked.

"No more questions, Bath," my mother said. The driver pulled up and my mother got out quickly and went to my father's side of the car, where I sat. She was next to me. He was gone, kicking in what remained of the front door.

"Do you want me to drop the bags?" the driver asked. My mother took my hand and pulled me out to stand up beside the car.

"Open the boot," she said. This struck me as strange, because she usually referred to it as the trunk. The driver looked confused, and my father came round and hit the button by the steering wheel. My mother grabbed the suitcases. I closed the trunk and saw my father's eyes in the outside rearview mirror. His lips moved, but I couldn't make out what he said, and the driver pulled away.

The house had been ransacked. Somehow they had gotten past the alarms and without alerting my father or his associates.

No one had come.

No one had checked.

There was a raccoon waiting for us on the kitchen counter.

I sometimes caught strange messages on my mother's phone. Nothing ever jumped out on the home screen. No notifications, but one day she left her phone open, because she'd had a friend on speaker when she went to the close the kitchen window. I had been sitting on the counter waiting for her to give me the car keys. A threatening-looking code ran across the top of the screen. The menace was not in the actual language, but in its subtext. New and real. At first glance it was unfamiliar, but then I was able to understand. It was similar to the sing-song stream of coordinates that came along with the shipping forecast. Not like other mothers' neighborhood gossip chains or group chats.

I knew I couldn't tell my mother that I'd been in her phone—she would have been furious. I had only just about been able to convince her that I needed to take my driver's test early. Any breach of her trust and respect would have been ill-advised. I also knew I would get more information by watching than by selling myself out.

So I pushed myself in further on the counter, my back to the wall. There was a bleach stain from months ago when the raccoon threw up everywhere. I pulled my right leg up and let my left foot dangle towards the floor. I tried to distract myself by watching my legs, the two black bracelets on my ankles, swiveling in opposite directions. Eyes unfocused, all I could see were shapes.

"Did the call drop?" my mother asked, walking back into the kitchen. "Stop that. What are you doing with your feet?"

"I think you lost her," I said, trying to be still. She picked up the phone and flicked into her messages. I knew she saw it because her hand became even more still. Spam? Some mothers got solicitations: coupons for chain supermarkets, or freelance job recruiters, or insurance pitches. My mother got unclear coordinates. "Aetna offer for those self-employed" hits differently when it comes after the above.

"Bath, what are you doing?"

"I need the keys."

"You can't drive alone yet."

"I know, will you come with me?" She was nodding her head, still looking down at her phone. I watched her walk to the closet and take out a baseball cap. The side table trembled when she picked up her sunglasses and purse. "What's wrong?"

"What do you mean?"

I shook my head and vaulted off the counter. "Nothing, let's go."

"What time do you have therapy?"

"Oh, I forgot. I think in an hour. Can we go drive after that?"

"Yes." I left her alone in the kitchen.

Ever since the party, and even more since coming home from France, my mother and my father had insisted I talk to the analyst. Whatever. There was no need. They persisted. I agreed. Tuesdays and Thursdays at 11 a.m. I did it because I was starting to see something that I wanted to understand, that there was a space where magic dovetailed with psychology.

When a psychic senses a story or an energy, it can be read like a kind of DSM-5. It gave me comfort to start to formulate some kind of system. The Latin study helped me with names, my sensitive hearing with sounds that weren't words. All hazy when applied to myself. I kept that part away, like my father's fat internist who told him to watch his cholesterol.

I could see these things in others. My method was still in formation, because I was both teacher and student. My peers were learning about science to grasp cause and effect.

Taking rational stabs at math and historic precedent to ace a test is so different from navigating a first unplanned fuck. I didn't have all the language—or perhaps too many languages, which made it harder. I had a sense of things, a sixth or seventh one. And I could hear winds or waves that no one else could. And I think my mother sensed what was coming and wanted to do all that she could to make sure it wouldn't destroy me. Not simply death, but to want it for myself.

Physical freedom: a driver's license was a kind of cover for letting me loose. It wouldn't interfere with whatever else was going on in my room. Strange mind. The therapy, I was sure, was a kind of surveillance into this. Not even seventeen, the analyst could report back to my parents. Knowing this, I was able to play with her a little, as well. Not out of malice, but because I knew I didn't want to be fully known by anyone.

I hadn't been able to articulate this before the party, but after that day, I knew. Even if you decide to live with just one or two close people, decide to circumscribe your world, you will receive strange messages and it will be hard to decode the way through.

I arranged my laptop to sit on the glass shelf in the middle of my vanity. "Hello, Bath." The analyst's voice came in along with her image. It wasn't the best setup, as I was sitting in front of both analyst and self in the mirror. I had also rigged my phone so that it would record the whole session, hidden so Dr. K. couldn't see. I kicked over the black cord on the floor.

"Hey." And then we both sat there in silence for three minutes. I liked to mess with her, knowing that unlike a regular therapist, she wasn't supposed to press with questions. Then I said, "I've been feeling really unsettled lately."

"Tell me about that."

"Like I want to run away, but not as an escape from this house. I love it here. It's a nest and safe and perfect. More like I want to run out of this life of mine in this body."

She stared at me. I changed the subject. "What I want to talk about is why other kids my age model themselves after these archetypes. Not like the classic kinds, but like the movie kind. For example, this gritty 80s drug lord, like in that French movie *The Professional*."

"Bathory."

"Yes, Dr. K?"

"Why don't you want to be known?"

"What do you mean?"

"You tell me."

"I want to talk to you about my theories. You're the only person who can help me with this. How would you feel about me having a psychic do a reading for me? And then you try to help me match up one-to-one the vision or tarot card that corresponds to a kind of subconscious impulse or childhood story."

"Your parents are paying a lot of money for you to talk to me."

"I don't want to talk about how I'm feeling. What helps me is to understand other people."

"It's your session."

"Semper hic adsum," I said, because she was pissing me off.

"What does that mean?"

"I am always here—near."

"Clever. You like learning Latin?"

I ignored her question. "My father hasn't been home in three weeks. I don't think he's ever coming home, and my mother gets death threats on her phone."

"Bathory. Come on now. This really isn't a joke."

"I'm serious."

"I think we should reconvene next week. I need to have a word with your parents." The small box where she had been went dark and she was gone. Where she had been, the outline of an old monastery-temple, my homepage wallpaper. A thick black box in the background of some kind of antiquity.

Our places in the car were finally reversed.

"Where do you want to go to celebrate?" my mother asked over the noise of the radio. Unlike her calm grip, my hands were clutching the steering wheel, my nails nearly piercing the tan leather, my elbows held high. She was smiling softly, looking at the road ahead as if she had one of those driving-school pedals on her side. It took my driver's permit turning into a full-blown license for me to see that the best way to explain my mother's walk through life after my birth was like this. As if she had a pedal, a safety hatch, which ensured she could eject before or around or in spite of whatever loose cannon fired. People, places and artillery.

"I just want to drive." She laughed and adjusted her sunglasses.

"Can we stop at the diner?"

"The one on Lincoln Drive?"

"Yes, do you know how to get there?"

"Straight here until the light?"

"Turn right at the second stoplight."

"How do you stay so calm all the time?"

"Because violence is inevitable."

"What? You didn't just say that?"

"I said, I imagine violins in tempo," she responded.

I shook my head at this. "I heard something else, sorry."

"Music is important, Bath." She was fucking with me.

"I know. It's all your fault."

"When you were a baby, you used to like Wagner. I always thought that was funny—prophetic."

"Prophetic?"

"A thought, one we can't yet know to be true."

"My brain doesn't keep to one line."

"If the line is not straight, it's still some kind of line."

"Why do you say 'some kind,' so much?"

"I guess it's an affect for effect."

"Ha ha."

"No, really. I can't be sure."

"But you so often seem sure."

"It's because I don't worry about anything except for two things."

"Which things?"

"You and your father." Neither of us addressed his prolonged absence. Instead, we went silent and listened to the calm accented voice of the shipping report. It had been playing like ambient music in the background of our entire conversation. After a strange blip, my mother reached out her left hand to flick the volume knob a full turn. The soothing voice hit differently at full blast. Still, the usual stream of unremarkable numbers, but something else, too, an ever so slight beep at rhythmic intervals. She quickly turned the other dial, and the station changed to a news broadcast in American English. "There has been a single-car crash on Interstate 95. A 1987 AMG Hammer," and then something I couldn't quite hear.

I could feel my mother get even more still than usual, like playing dead. She put her right hand on the back of her hat, as if to be sure it was there, angling her neck forward, looking past me through the driver's side window. We drove together like that until I turned at the light. "This is the first time you've delivered me anywhere," she said as I put the car in park. "Insane timing. Well, I've officially handed something over to you."

"I like it here," Iggy said, picking up his burger with both hands, looking directly at the meat.

"My mother took me here right after I got my license."

"When was that? Yesterday?"

"Very funny."

"No, really."

"Like a year ago. Before we found out about my father." I had been looking directly at him until I said it aloud. "I mean, found out that we weren't going to find out."

"I want to talk to you about that," Iggy said, pressing his tongue into his cheek.

I nodded. "Remind me what you have to do at the museum?" I had been waiting for his visit for so long.

"Have you seen the archives there?"

"I actually haven't been."

"I'm going to take you, but not before you eat that." I hadn't touched my omelet.

"I can't believe they let you into that place for research," I said.

"What do you mean?"

"Your kind aren't welcome there." He laughed.

"The opposite. I know where things are that they want, and even better: I know how to make them. Don't you remember that painting hanging over the entryway to the back room?"

"Not really."

"The Rembrandt that hung near the fireplace. It is his only painted seascape."

"You aren't supposed to hang masterpieces close to open flames."

"Well, exactly."

"I remember now: with the men trying to keep control of the fishing boat in the storm."

"Some kind of magic." He took three French fries between his fingers and held them up. It was summertime weather; school would end in a week. He still had on one of his long-sleeved T-shirts. The wrist of his left hand had somehow gotten ketchup on the cuff. He saw this, and looking back over his right shoulder, pushed up the dirty sleeve. I tried not to look.

"My father mentioned the painting the last time I saw him."

"Oh, really?"

"Yeah, crazy I forgot about that."

Something flashed across his face. "I need to run to the restroom," he said, and got up quickly, leaving his phone behind. I noticed it as soon as he was out of sight, sitting on top of his laptop. He'd had both out and was working when I arrived.

Before I could yell to him, he had already realized. He came back to the table, paused, and then opened his computer, quickly typing the password to read something. He seemed to log in and then left, phone in hand, for the toilet.

For no reason other than it felt a little dangerous and I was annoyed, I opened his computer. When I touched the keyboard, the screen lit up. It was still unlocked, his i-message open.

The last text chain showed the bottom of a picture Iggy had sent of a target: a red rectangle that had eaten a gray oval with a dark gray rectangle inside both, the same shape as the larger one. There were bullet holes like starbursts near the center. The person he was texting with had written "haha" to his text and

"AK-47

It is."

Then there was another image of the same target with classic holes near the center. And below Iggy had typed, ".385 revolver."

"357

Or 38.

There is no such thing as a 358 revolver.

Probably a 367 with 38 specials in it

There is a 380 but not in a revolver," read the response.

Then Iggy again: "38"

"Nice. Left-handed or right-handed?" A graphic showing some kind of rubric, a circle. Then, "If using right hand to pull trigger. If left-handed the chart is opposite

Or sights off a bit."

Iggy responded. "What am I doing wrong with my right?"

Then, "You are not used to a revolver trigger

Heavy and lots of creep."

I thought I heard Iggy's voice and looked behind me. He wasn't there, but I knew I should close the computer. I had been so mesmerized that I hadn't checked the name at the top: "Captain Will."

It took Iggy forty-five minutes to return from the bathroom. By then, I had finished my cold omelet and eaten a few of the remaining fries as well.

"Will you drive me home now? I paid the bill," I said.

"Yeah, okay." He knew he had been extremely rude and that he needed to give me an explanation. But he also knew that I was used to this kind of situation, not knowing. I felt him looking at me the same way he had that day on our failed ice cream mission. Every mission we shared had failed. The party was the real failure. What happened that night that neither he nor Captain Will talked about, let alone had prevented. The bid for ice cream and now our cut-short burger date. Still, I knew there was something that tethered us together, and it was none of the things that had or hadn't happened.

"My father once explained to me that I should question all the images all over your house, and that this included your mother."

"Well, they are both gone now."

I followed him out to the car.

Before we got on the plane to New York, my mother insisted that we go to the diner. The restaurant had become a kind of movie set or novelistic device in my life. She drove us there, Wagner on the radio, baseball hat on, unbothered, which was not always the tip-off it seemed to be. When we got to the parking lot, she locked the doors.

"What are you doing?" I asked.

"I need to talk to you before we go inside."

My bags were in the trunk. We only had an hour before heading to Logan. "What do you want to talk about?"

"The family business."

"There's a family business?"

"Not like that."

"What do you mean?"

"There's no big company or fund. The opposite."

"A major debt?" She laughed and shook her head.

"Before your father's death was confirmed, I told you he'd gone missing on his business trip to South America, and you said something to me. Do you remember?"

"It was so fucked up the things you kept from me."

"Yes, but what did you say?"

"I don't remember. Something like 'You and your parental withholding, you act like he's an assassin.'"

"He was."

"Excuse me?"

"So was his father and his brothers and I think his father's father."

"And you?"

"My own kind."

"Your own kind. Why didn't you kill me when you had the chance?"

"I don't kill people." She said it not as judgment but to emphasize it wasn't her particular job.

"What do you do, then?"

"Something like espionage and triage."

"Oh."

"I thought you sort of knew."

"Nah, I took you at your word."

"I never lie."

"What do you mean?"

"It's how I keep things straight. You'd be surprised. Conversation lends itself to elision. Not everyone uses this tactic, of course."

"You don't really teach sometimes?"

"I do." I laughed. She said, "I run something called the Latin Research Foundation—that's the name most of the time."

"What does this mean?"

"You get to chase whatever you want now."

"Oh, I see," I said, acknowledging her riddles, her truths by omission. She was delivering facts. Turns out, she always had been.

74

"There are some people your father wanted you to talk to once you turned eighteen. They are all in New York." I thought about asking her about Iggy, but such a discussion felt somehow already like a betrayal of both.

"How will I find them?"

"They will get in touch with you."

The scout told me to come to a place on Grand Street. I was disheveled and confused, but a little cash would be helpful. And maybe it would lead to a gig that could bring me downtown on the regular. If it wasn't a modeling agency, but another kind, I'd deal with that inevitability.

When I arrived at the address given to me, there was a woman with wide-set eyes smoking outside. She saw me out of the corner of her eye and slumped against the wall, pretending not to. It had to be an act, because of the way her feet were turned, and the way her hands trembled as she lit each cigarette. "I love a chain smoker in this day and age," I said to her. She laughed and offered her hand. "I'm Caroline. People call me Caro."

"I'm Margot." I didn't trust her.

"Want a cigarette?"

"Yes, please." She handed me a thin, unopened pack with the warning written in French in a block on the bottom and her feet turned towards me. There were ratty pink ribbons hanging out of her bag. I pointed to them. "You dance?"

She nodded. "I'm about to give it up."

"For modeling?"

"You could say that."

"What do you mean?"

"I meet men sometimes." Unsolicited admission, easy tell. It came out as if she, too, had been waiting for the correct stranger to show up.

"That's cool." She motioned for me to hand her back the pack. Unwrapping it with her teeth, she took out a single cigarette. I expected her to offer it to me, but instead she kept it as a standby until she'd smoked what was left of the other.

"I have a friend who is a really famous, I mean completely mind-blowingly famous, K-pop–style singer. She's transcended the genre now." I nodded for her to go on while interrupting her: "May I have a cigarette?" She handed me the one she had been twirling between her fingers. "I know this band, Black Throne, doesn't exactly sound like what you imagine it to be."

"Yeah, the lead singer is Mary Cosossart."

Caro waved me off. "She started in that super group and yesterday announced she's leaving to have a solo career and start her own entertainment company. Her next single drops in two weeks. She said I could be the creative director," Caro said this and then, to be sure I understood, "I'll have a title. It was my convincing that made her finally do it. She trusts me; I was at Juilliard before."

"You quit?"

"I told you already. Look, I'm not dumb. I get how it all works. All anyone wants is to know I was a ballerina at Juilliard. And then I'll fuck you." She blew out a circle of smoke. "Mary is pre-Hollywood, before she gets in the ring. She needs creative control."

"The ring? Like Rocky?"

"The stage."

"She's leaving the stage?"

Caro opened her eyes as wide as she could. "Stepping onto the grand stage." She shifted her feet. "She's literally a superstar. Everyone wants to meet her, be around her, close to her. What's strange is simultaneously she's having some kind of crisis, telling me she only has a year."

"Like she's terminally ill?"

"Hahah—no." She sucked in smoke and went on, "Mary tells me one night when she's really drunk or high, I can never tell which, that her actual goal is to lock down a French guy from some family. That's the ring." I started to laugh.

"Two options."

"Two families. Lots of sons."

Caro was pure entertainment herself. Explaining away something like one would the military-industrial complex, but with young pop phenoms. The kind that years ago would have visited the troops as star entertainers.

I was into human folly without investment. Detachment; not destiny. "What's your phone number?" I asked her. "I have to go soon."

"My name is spelled C-A-R-O, like the syrup but with a 'C.' Short for Caroline." She said this as if making sure of it herself, then handed me her own phone after hitting in the passcode, cigarette balanced between two fingers. "Put yours in here and then call it."

I gave her one of the two numbers I had in rotating use. It made it easier to keep things straight, even before there was reason for them to be messy. My mother had helped me sort this out at the local tech shop back home. She'd also put Iggy's number as one of the contacts on the first-tier phone number, but I hadn't dared to call it.

"Margot—with a 'T,'" I told Caro, but then decided it was better to mention my real name, if only to help keep it all straight myself. "Some people call me 'Bat' like with a 'T,' but it's spelled without—I mean it's spelled 'B-A-T-H,' like a porcelain tub with claw feet."

"Put yourself in as whatever you want," she said, uninterested, still holding the last of her cigarette.

The modeling agency called me later to say they wanted me and had some big job in Paris. I declined. When you're taught as a child not to covet fame, you never want to be the one watched. All eyes off.

Modeling scout, my ass. Life gives you a decoy so when the real thing comes, you recognize it.

I hated living uptown. There was really no need for me to be there. I could take the train to go to class. I hated school. Most of the other women were super wound-up, thinking that their secret societies were the real thing. Alyssa had decided to go to school in New Paltz, which wasn't all that far, but far enough to feel.

I spent as much time as I could below 14th, although there was one cultural-theory guy, with all his complex complexes, who was fairly fascinating to me and who kept his activities in the triple-digit streets. He loved the library, and it was my job to help him desecrate this sacred place. He told me that he could sense I was coming at him at 0.5, the other co-ed prospects at 10. And he hated that he couldn't intellectualize what was happening: what would happen.

"Why are you like this?" he asked me one day when I was pulling on my shirt behind the J's.

"Like what?"

"Not upset."

I started laughing, then realized I had to be quiet, because people were studying. "Why would I be upset?"

"Because I didn't ask you to hang out later or this weekend."

"I can't hang out. I have to work." He nodded and looked down. I continued, "You are upset that I'm not upset, because you didn't do something that you had no intention to do?"

"I'm fine," he said, and I laughed again.

"I'm not gonna give you what you want," I said, staring him down. "Why set it up so you'll have to grieve someone you didn't have to attach to in the first place?"

"Like you're gonna die?"

"No, like a breakup." I was careful not to roll my eyes.

School was easy. Phone-it-in easy. Men like the theorist were more interesting; it was through sex that I was able to learn. Street smarts were something that had eluded me as a teenager for the exact reason I should have had them. So I spent college trying to learn the rules.

Those who make the rules don't care about the rules.

I knew when someone was tethered to me, both by sight and initiation. Or "site," a better spelling to explain this. On the ground, IRL, 3D, I can sense something immediately. The staying alive, free will, and codes of conduct all raise interference. And school scrambles things. Cultural theory guy was so much more useful than any professor. I called him Professor, in fact, which he liked. I started speaking Latin to him, which he didn't understand. Mostly clichés, because he was one, too. All of us—there were two others, an Ancient Greek graduate student and a policeman I met at the bodega where he was buying an energy drink.

"Heyyyyy," I said to the man behind the counter.

"Moon," he smiled back. I could only see only the right side of his upturned mouth, the rest of it obscured by a stack of fireballs. Overhead, a quilt of single-dose drug packets: pink, white, red, blue, and yellow. I nodded and waved dramatically so I could see myself on the surveillance monitor.

"Why does he call you Moon?" A haunted male voice behind me asked. I looked up at the screen and saw a figure in a dark blue uniform. He was so tall, his head was cut off. I turned around.

"Because he only sees me once a month," I said. The uniformed man was two days unshaven; his eyes looked as if he'd been awake even longer. He was very handsome and smelled like metal and cigarettes. "I don't get it," he said, pointing to the smokes behind the counter. "The moon's out every night."

"I think he means like a full moon," I said, looking down before turning to walk towards the freezer case. He followed me down the next aisle, eventually stepping in front of me. "What—"

"I need some detergent," he said.

"Detergent? Don't they clean your uniforms?"

He laughed. "I was just following you."

"You know there's a camera up there."

"You're not very friendly."

"You're in my way," I said, trying to walk past him.

"Would you have a coffee with me?"

"I want a water," I said, bending down.

"I'll take you out for water."

"Don't you have laundry to do?" He was between the chips and candies, staring at me on my knees in front of the energy drinks. I couldn't help but laugh at the stupid look of delight on his face. "Fine."

"Thank you," he said, offering his hand. "I'm Danny."

"Danny?"

"Yeah."

"Are you fifteen?" I asked, standing up and letting go.

"Jesus Christ."

"Sorry, sorry."

"What's your name?"

"Bathory."

"I give up." He shook his head.

"No, really."

"Like the band?"

"Yeah."

"You're intense," he said. "Moon. Bathory. What?" I shrugged.

"I don't date cops."

"I don't date witches."

"What?"

"What's your real name?"

"Bath."

"Like in baseball?"

I ignored the question. "How does it work, that line between your personal and professional life?"

"Same as it does for you."

"You don't know what I do."

"Tell me then."

"I—I teach Latin."

"Where?"

"I run this thing called the Latin Research Foundation."

"People still care about that?"

"They do." He nodded his head.

"Where is it?"

"We meet different places—with different people—depending on need."

"We're going for a coffee across the street," he said, grabbing my hand. "Take this," he said to the man behind the register, handing him the blue drink I'd been holding.

"Bye, Moon," the clerk said as the door slammed.

My detachment only seemed to make them come harder. Notes under my dorm room door. Emails, so many emails. I told them not to text me and never to signal me on any kind of social media. I rarely checked it anyway. They all thought I was super private, which was true, but also I could feel even the digital message thinking itself clever. "Don't ever send me song lyrics unless you write them yourself, and even then think hard."

I spent my Tuesdays in the library reading old Latin manuscripts until the grad student came to find me; Wednesday mornings walking home from the precinct; and Thursdays in the park for half the day and the other half with grad student number two in his apartment. Sometimes on Fridays we'd go downtown to the movies. Weekends ended on Monday. Having a schedule calmed me down. I wasn't dealing with any one I loved.

I completed all my coursework two years in, all the while managing to make it through with no close female friends. Caro was, like romance, only entertainment. I had been so isolated as a teenager living outside Boston that I'd never felt the need for many acquaintances. I had listened to my mother: I had her, my father—sometimes—and Alyssa. College confirmed this twofold. I'd never seen so many young people hopped up on false ideals and goal posts, visible in one way, invisible in another. It didn't take long for me to promise myself that I would remain detached.

It's hard to read all those online signals—even just an email—but if ancient linguistics, including hermetic energies, are your thing, you can hear electronic code too, music, dialect, vernacular, affect, and shared history. Intuition for visitations or images is inverse to real life. Be saved endlessly any given day.

Why didn't anyone ever tell these fools that going public is giving away your power?

I was supposed to have another year in the city, but I had all my credits secured and my Latin was perfect. Really, it had been when I was seven. And so when the messenger arrived with his strange summons I had no further questions. Hellfire couldn't get me to apply for an internship.

It was almost a year after the modeling scout stopped me on the street that an old man signaled me in the park. He looked a lot like my father. I can't tell you if that's because everyone looks or looked like him at some point, or my father had endeavored to look like all men. Either way, it's not so hard to look like someone's presumed-dead father. A tick, a gait, a barely audible sound, steady hands; it's worse when it could be him. When you're shy of twenty-two and you still can't shake seeing Kobe Bryant memorabilia, it's likely he's still alive somewhere. My father had told me that he always would be, at the very least, watching. ("Like the Internet, Bath.") A promise that he would be there everywhere all at once. ("Like a good story.")

"Bathory," the old man said when he walked by, looking down at me. I patted my chest and made sure I was still wearing the orange-and-tan jacket I'd put on that morning. Nothing else on me referenced an identity. I kept walking for a few seconds and then went and sat on the bench on the sidewalk outside the park. He came and sat next to me, didn't say anything, and took out his phone to tap it against his knee. I looked down and he had a text-message window open. My name was in the To: box, flashing cursor at the end. He hadn't pressed Send. There would be no trace of the message in which he'd typed the address:

"55 E 77th St."

I put my hand on top of his hand so that I could see it clearly, and took out my phone to take a picture. "How's your day going?" I asked. He laughed and smiled.

"Beautiful here," he said. "Gotta go." And he just got up and walked away.

"Wait," I said, but he ignored me. His right hand fell behind him, two middle fingers to thumb, pointer and pinkie in the air. I laughed. Good-bye: an upside-down death metal sign. Unintentional or otherwise, it was there.

I no longer rode shotgun while listening to someone tell me things that would change the course of my life. Open-air, big city, it could happen anywhere.

After the man was out of sight, I received a message: 23 hr.

I was to be at 55 East 77th Street that evening. Eleven p.m.

And there was Iggy, three years later. He was wearing a short-sleeved T-shirt from a neighborhood bar over a black long-sleeved T-shirt and navy corduroys. Murky lamplight caught the city dust before breaking into the sewer grill. Iggy stood still, clocking my presence. His clothes were lit up in particle-filled smoke, the inverse of a chalk-outline murder scene. In his absence, he'd fused with what I'd learned the last time we'd seen each other. That my father was alive and communicating, but dead to me. Resurrection; always a resurrection with Iggy. With all the men I cared about. In privilege, some of the others lost purpose. No war to die for.

Iggy and I both understood the assignment, and walked in single file, phantom-directed to the same address. He pushed the door in with his shoulder. I followed him. We hadn't formally acknowledged one another until he reached his hand back to me on the stairs. I took it and realized he had been there before. Unsteady, I let go and tried to put my hand on his back when we reached the landing. He allowed it, held it there, to tell me we were back in touch and safe. None of the other men I'd been with felt protective. Only of themselves.

I let go and fell behind him, staying under the thick part of the stairs. He knocked on the door, three raps. Eventually someone opened it, and he walked in alone. When he came out moments later, he held a key in his right hand. I didn't know if I should wait or follow him, and watched until he made a move. He kept putting his free hand in his corduroy pocket as if looking for something that wasn't there to begin with.

Finally, he started up the stairs again, gesturing for me to follow. Six more flights. It was difficult to see. Sad, slow harp music came up from the ground floor. He stopped in front of 9C and put the key in the lock. The door gave way. He held his other hand out for me.

It was darker in the apartment than outside. I turned on my phone's flashlight and Iggy batted it down, but not before I saw that the ceiling and walls were painted navy. I ran my hand along the perimeter of the room. Iggy lit a match, the same way he had in the grotto. Pulled from nowhere and just on time.

We entered a second chamber. It wasn't exactly a room, because the space was laid out like a loft sectioned in three. There was a mattress on the floor; Iggy appeared to taste the air, then sat on it, his back against the wall. He put something between his fingers and it ignited, and then he motioned for me to join him. A fresh sheet had been stretched over the mattress, so that when I sat down, a familiar smell was sent into the air. "Bath?" Iggy said.

"Iggy." He laughed and stood the torch base on the floor.

"Here we are again. You still go by Bath?"

"What else?"

"I thought maybe you'd have a new name for school."

"Margot?"

"That's it."

"How did you know?" He shrugged. "How's Captain Will?"

"Will?"

"Good old free Will. I know he's alive. I'm so tired of you guys pretending I don't get it."

"No one's pretending."

"You think I don't understand?"

"That's not what I meant," he said, smiling at how combative I was. "I think we all understand that you see everything and translate the signs. This isn't limited to linguistics."

"'We all'? Who is this committee?" He hadn't stopped looking at me with that strange smile. His eyes closed a little as he let out a sound, a single soft release of air, his version of a laugh. It was like he'd set free some built-up steam when he broke from his usual poker face. "You barely know me." He tilted his head and smiled, then looked down.

"I assumed you were like your mother. She's legendary for her ability to see things that no one else can see."

"When I was little, I thought this meant animals. I mean, it did. It seemed like she was always able to find them and point them out to me."

"That's sweet, and a funny side effect of her skill set. She told me once that her daughter was better at reading the signs than she'd ever been."

"When did you see her?"

"Remember when you came to visit?" He was fumbling his words.

"That long ago?"

"I mean, I've seen her since then." I didn't press him. "Translation, though. That is your thing, right?"

"I guess so." He laughed.

"Apropos tonight," he started, then stopped himself. "*Apropos* is Latin, no?"

"Seventeenth-century French, but yeah, a few hundred years earlier Latin origin."

"You can even do two steps removed."

I laughed again and shook my head, "That's a funny way to say it."

"Semantics," he said, waving me away and cracking the same smile. He forgot about his earlier thought and put his arm around me. I didn't have a chance to register it, save for the fall in my stomach. The sparring was admission. Joint consensus on both things. We were old-new. Still, at the beginning, it's always an opportunity to wipe something clean. Then, the off chance that it's permanent.

"Iggy is a dumb name." We'd both forgotten how we'd gotten there.

"At least I'm not named after a serial killer." As he said this, I took off my sweater.

"Bathory is a great name. Both band and witch."

"And weapon," he said. I looked at him for as long as I could before I became uncomfortable. Not in the way of feeling uneasy, because something was wrong, but uneasy in the other way. There had to be a word for that, when something makes you uneasy because it's familiar and correct, and everything else is not.

It was dark, but I could see Iggy's naked forearm, which he usually kept hidden. Fallen vigilance that found us exposed, in some strange bed. I could see that the scar was hard and raised, running from below his wrist almost to his elbow. He startled me by pulling off his trainers and throwing them across the room. I laughed and took mine off too.

"It is important for us to be warm and open with one another," he said.

"Warm?"

"I mean, clear."

"So now you believe in transparency?"

"What does that mean?" I realized he was half teasing, half serious.

"It's funny, you still assume I keep myself out of trouble and my head in books."

"Old scrolls." I hit him playfully. "I don't assume anything, especially since you look like that," he said.

"I'm a fully formed human being like you."

"You don't look human to me." He made a face that suggested he was unsure. "Nymph, maybe." I put my hand on his lower stomach below his T shirt. He didn't move, but I felt suddenly unsafe.

"I'm not normal," I said, and he started laughing.

"I have no idea what that means. Fighting and fucking are so much more important."

He somehow lifted me while lying down, so that I was sitting over him and he could see my face. Trying to keep steady, I fixed on his eyes, which were not gentle, but large and full of rage, but not for me. It was what led him to want to get rid of something. I took my own shirt off and then his, putting them both on the floor next to our mattress. He smiled and lifted me back off so that he could get undressed. I did the same. Even through this solo we kept our eyes turned towards each another. He watched me, and his face signaled what I could only decode as great expectation and steadfast tenderness. One empty delusion-derangement—and the promise to hold it down, make it whole. I didn't mind the eyes. His eyes watching everything. My solitary undressing was part of the dance. And then when we were both naked, staring at one another, fixed in the half-moon light, he flipped me over onto him all at once.

"So why did we meet tonight?" I asked. He smiled. "The Agency has a sense of humor, but I'm not sure they are free with these kind of connections."

"Which agency?"

"There is no name, we just say that."

"I see."

"I am supposed to give you this," he picked up his corduroys and pulled something rectangular out of the pocket. Two other pieces of paper fell out at the same time. "I was so worried I would lose this. Here," he said, handing it to me.

It was a sports card, preserved between two thin pieces of plastic. "Kobe Bryant: Lower Merion H.S. (PA.)" on the front. The back was covered with a piece of paper someone had slid inside. Iggy pulled on his pants and found my shirt to hand to me. "I should go," he said, as I reached over to help collect the fallen contents of his pocket: There was a candy wrapper and a box of toothpicks. I handed both back to him. I was still completely naked, standing in the dark.

"Where?"

"I fly out this evening," he said.

"I thought you lived here now."

"I don't live anywhere." I stood up and looked at him. He turned away. "I'll find you someplace sometime," he said. I was upset at him.

"What happened to your wrist?" I asked him, to prevent myself from saying what I wanted to say.

"I'll tell you next time."

"I get it, you don't know me very well."

"Look, I'm not going very far." He stopped before the door and turned around.

"'Scio te mihi futurum esse.' That's right, no?"

"I don't think so. Unless you meant to say, 'I know you. I always have.'"

The subway ride uptown was interminable. Two men tried to sit next to me and twice I had to get up and go across the way. I smelled of sex. It took me fifteen minutes to find four orange chairs without anyone nearby.

I pulled the paper out from behind the card. It was only a receipt, proof of payment for the rookie card, time stamped just a few days prior. Bought at a place called Card Town located on Avenue A between Third and Fourth Streets in the East Village. It was my father reborn, confirming he was alive. Relief and great disappointment.

The comedown from Iggy's appearance felt heavier than I had expected. His quick, certain exit made it clear there was no next move. But that was a false claim, because a playbook can read one way and you can still sense the truth. It had happened only once between us, a crazy basis to assume proprietary status. Crazier because I was committed to detachment. And still, it was there.

I put the basketball card away in my purse. Strange to have a paper receipt in such a day and age. Overcome with exhaustion, I slept the rest of the train ride.

Three weeks passed and I didn't hear from Iggy. I knew I shouldn't be the one to write. He wouldn't answer. And then on the twenty-second day I got a text from the number my mother had put in my phone.

"I figured it out:
Conans viam reperire
sed semper hic ades.
In case I'm wrong:
Just trying to find my way
But you're always here."

I agreed to meet Matthew at my favorite dinner place, mainly because he hadn't given up after that day outside Latin class. He was another graduate student, an older one. The Greek guy—he was actually from Minneapolis—was only four years my senior. This one had more than a decade on me. He told me he'd decided to leave Wall Street to study classics. I told him it was lame to go from finance to humanities. Used to applause, he liked that. I didn't respond to his first three text messages, and so he asked a fourth time. I said "Fine," and told him to meet me at a sushi place downtown.

"Do you want a beer?" I asked as he sat down next to me in the booth.

"Whisky, please."

"Oh, sure, the waitress will be right back." He was wearing a blue button-down, jeans, and gray old-man sneakers, the same as the man who had signaled to me outside the park. "You look nice."

"Thank you," he said. "How was your day?"

"It was fine. I've been spending a lot of time in the library," I said. "I need to decide what's next soon."

"What are you thinking?"

"I'll either become a translator or an assassin."

"That's funny." I nodded and smiled without showing my teeth. "So what do you get here?"

"Sushi," I said, wrapping the thick paper napkin around my forefinger.

"You are very funny."

I looked down at my ankles.

"You should see the last guy I came here with."

"Oh really?"

I nodded again, tapping my fingers. The spiraled napkin landed next to my Japanese beer.

"You know what's a mind fuck, dating a famous Italian rapper." I couldn't help myself.

"What?"

"That's who I was here with." It was true. Caro had set me up with him when he came to town. I agreed for the same reasons I hung out with her, a natural extension of the psyop-and-smoke nature of our friendship. "Some people are famous in one country and not at all in another, and it's wild to watch."

He signaled the waitress and asked for another whisky. "Like they come over here and go into a restaurant like this and expect to be recognized, but the context is gone."

"Like when I had to get up at 3 a.m. to work the foreign markets."

I paused and considered this. "No." I continued, "It would be different even if he was an actor who carried personas with him, but he was the persona. All day long. The man moved his lips when he read a menu."

"Did I show you my tattoo?" Matthew asked. I considered walking out.

"No."

"I will later."

"Oh, okay," I said. He didn't seem to care that he had stopped me mid-story.

"So where did you grow up?"

"North Dakota," I said.

"I used to date a girl from North Dakota."

"Oh yeah?" I had thought I could fake it long enough to fuck him, to see what it was like.

"Big oil family." I motioned for the waitress.

"Good idea, I need another one and let's order." She came over to my side of the table. I motioned for her to come closer, covering my mouth with my right hand as if relaying a secret.

I got up and threw the paper snake at him before I walked out.

On the taxi ride home I looked at Iggy's last message. It took that dinner for me to know. Given the right circumstances, I could do it. Provoke and bolt. Set the groundwork for someone else. Be a good Platonian demon to set traps and make mischief if certain loyalties were clear.

I asked the driver if we could reroute, turn right around.

"Of course," he said. "You are my passenger. I work for you."

"Can you drop me at Card Town?"

"I've been working around here for fifty years, and I've never heard of that. What's the address?"

"Forty-seven Avenue A, between East Third and Fourth," I said. And he quietly drove me there.

It was 8:08 when I got out of the cab. I tipped the man $20 as good luck, more for me than him. He had been right; it wasn't called Card Town. Stock Stationers. There was a thick foggy mint-green strip on the window, from the edge of the door to the shop's far side. Above it, letters spelled out the name. I pushed the door open and a sound went off, signaling my arrival. The sign said the shop closed at 8 p.m.

The air smelled funny, unlike the stationery story on University Place. Not old paper, but a gasoline-like scent. The linoleum on the ceiling was lifted at certain corners, familiar black wires creeping out. No one behind the counter, the only sound the faint whirring of an electronic toy diver in a little box of water on the floor who kept hitting his head as he tried to go forward. I lifted him dripping onto a shelf next to baby-blue deodorant. There were only two of each cosmetic or foodstuff, the items stacked in short rows, not unlike a shop Iggy had taken me to way back in France. No sign of sports cards or collectibles anywhere. Only bootleg laundry detergent, hair elastics, and gummy candy.

I ran my hand along the metal stacks and some of the makeshift price tags fell on the floor. When I bent down to pick them up, I noticed that the bottom shelves were all empty. The stationery supplies were limited to a graphic-printed plastic cup filled with basic blue ballpoint pens and greeting cards mixed in a cardboard box. "Happy Birthday to my Daughter," on top of "Condolences!" underneath "Happy Golden Anniversary Baby Girl."

"Can I help you?" The voice from the back of the shop was strangely familiar.

My instinct was to get him to show himself. "I need some help."

"Coming." A very tall fifty-something man emerged. "It's you," he said when he saw me. "Finally." I couldn't quite place him. "You look so much like your mother." He smiled and looked at the ceiling and then waved his hand. "Quick, come into the back." I followed him through an orange-and-red bead curtain to a metal door. "As you know, the shop is a front."

"I'm confused, was it once a sports store or always a stationer?"

"Always a stationer." The Kobe card had been my father's special touch. My guide opened the door, revealing a card table set up with three folding chairs.

"Do you want a drink?" the man asked.

"I just had three Japanese beers."

"Are you in your head?"

"Like am I struggling or am I drunk?"

"A pair of fair questions."

"I'm not drunk, and I think what I was struggling with is starting to be explained."

"Go on," he said, and politely pulled out one of the chairs for me.

"A card table. Classic," I said.

"This is your Card Town."

"Just playing the hand that was dealt." I couldn't help myself. "So, I'm in the back of a front."

"So much like your mother," he said, shaking his head and smiling again.

"You talk to her?"

"Yes, I do."

"What does that look like?"

"We speak on the phone."

"Right." I pushed myself a little further back from the table. There was a black stain on one quarter of the table's light wood grain. "And my father?"

He paused, weighing what to say. "How did you get here." It was not a question.

I nodded. "What do you want from me?"

"I need a store clerk."

"What?"

"Really, I need someone to work the register. Someone who is young and elegant and not like the other guys who work for me."

I laughed. "This is not what I expected."

"Well, we all felt you didn't want all in."

"No, I've been waiting for this for years."

"Yes, well, you knew it was coming. That's the thing. The opposite of opportunism. You don't get to make it personal."

"Right. What should I know?"

"Right now, your shifts. When do you have class?"

"Mondays and Fridays but at different times."

"We will open Wednesday and Thursday from 9 a.m. to 7 p.m."

"Only two days a week?"

"I'll figure out the other days. Do you have any friends?"

I couldn't figure out if this was a general question or a test. "I have no real friends. There are three guys I see every now and then."

"No friends?"

"I know people. I hang out with them—there's this one girl Caro and another named Alyssa, but she lives upstate."

"What do they do?"

"Caro is a dancer and an escort and Alyssa is an actress-writer."

"The men?"

"Two—maybe three—are grad students and one is a police officer." He stopped smiling.

"Get rid of the last one."

"He could be useful."

"It's not worth the risk. Unless you love this guy."

"I don't love anyone."

"Are you in touch with John's son?"

"Iggy?"

He nodded and I nodded back. "Here's what I can tell you," he said. "This can go as far as you want, but you need to start with the shop." I couldn't tell if he was talking about Iggy or my professional path. Maybe both. "Say it's a part-time retail gig to anyone who asks." He got up from the table and walked to a safe at the back of the room.

"No one is going to ask."

"You'd be surprised. That's the universe: Once there's a secret, people ask."

"I know about this stuff."

"Bath, everything is about to change."

"I've heard that before."

"Have you?"

"I guess not, but it's happened before."

"I'm going to overstep here, because I know Will would want me to." I was shocked to hear my father's name said aloud and said with high intensity.

"I've met you before . . ." I interrupted him. He stopped what he was doing and turned around to look at me in a way that signaled I shouldn't go on.

"Komodo dragon," he said, then turned back toward the safe and went on, "I know you can handle discomfort, but from here on out only do what you're comfortable with—however that shakes out in your body, your 'feelings' is up to you. Forget all that therapy—"

"Analysis," I said.

"Same thing. Our kind, we need to see beyond that sort of nonsense. For example, a guru will tell you to go towards a new version of a bad situation to set it straight, while a Western shrink will tell you the opposite. Best to heed neither. Anyway, like I said, everything is about to change.

"You can't mastermind this moment. An accident. A shot. One seems planned, but they have the same kinetics. I don't need to tell you that. Your mother already did." He paused and unwrapped something. "Hocus-pocus, I mean. I don't understand Latin." He turned around and handed me a metal ring hung with seven keys. "This one is for the store," he said, separating one and then tossing the entire chain into my lap. "You know, I went to school up there, too."

"What did you study?"

"Very little, but I ran a quite successful gambling ring out of the library."

"I have kind of a similar thing going. We call it the Latin Research Society."

He nodded. "Be careful." He said it in such a loving, regretful way, that I got up and reached my hand out to him. At first, he balked, looked uncomfortable, then halved the energy by starting to laugh. "What a thing to say," he said, making fun of himself as he took my hand across the table.

"Be careful is perfect," I said, and turned his hand over in mine.

"Did you ever hear—see?—that joke circulating online about the wealthy kid from far away who went to study up there, too. He wrote a letter to his father: 'Dad, school is epic, but I feel silly when I arrive at University in my Maserati, while the professors come by train.' He received a letter back from his father with a check for 30 million. 'Buy yourself a train, my son, and don't embarrass us in front of foreigners.'" I started to laugh and put both my hands flat on the table, leaving the keys in my lap.

"No, it's funny. And it's stupid. I'm telling you now because everything is both. Remember that. You should head out now. There's a cab waiting for you outside."

"A cab?"

"Yeah, don't ask. Or about Iggy."

"What?"

"Welcome home, Bath," he said, and got up and left through the metal door. I followed him out.

Two months after I was hired at Card Town another message came from Iggy: "Our biology isn't equipped to contend with virtual approximation." And as if he sensed I needed more and knew not to answer, he added, "I should be with you today." I knew better than to ask for details or expect them. This was the wager: to believe in a connection that rarely showed itself. We'd been together only once, a grounded counterpoint. It was the kind of thing you'd replay with a good friend over and over, but I didn't have any friends like that. I'd known Caro for a year now and I didn't trust her. I had known Iggy for longer in years, but not in moments. Still, none of that changed the stakes.

Caro was great because she saw things I didn't see, for the very reasons I kept my distance. She consumed the world around her in a way that excited and terrified me. I had ended things as instructed with the police officer, by telling him I needed to focus on my work; I was starting a Latin research foundation. He said he understood and to call him whenever I needed anything. Like any good law enforcement agent, he didn't ask what the Latin Research Foundation was or care that I might refer to it on any given day as the International Latin Society: ILS. And he only asked to fuck me one last time. I said, "No, thank you," took one of his NYPD sweatshirts, and walked out.

His scheduled mornings now belonged to Caro. She and I would meet at a coffee shop on the Lower East Side, always the first people there, her alibi when she had to leave a man she wanted to get away from. Most often they were clients, sometimes they were chosen lovers, sometimes it was hard to tell the difference.

"You don't look so good," I said. She was wearing a gray hoodie over a long tight black dress with flat sandals that laced up her calves. The whole look, while far more elegant than usual, seemed awry. When she arrived, she was holding the hem of her dress in one hand, an unlit cigarette in the other.

"Not the best night," she said.

"Let's go outside and you can smoke and tell me all about it."

"Yeah, let me get a coffee first."

"You want your usual?" I asked. "I have to go to work in an hour." She nodded and I walked into the shop, ordered a classic drip, a triple espresso, and a double for myself. It was one of Caro's better traits, that she only believes in one kind of milk: the cow kind. When I came out, drinks in hand, I couldn't find her at first. Then I noticed her across the street, folded into her phone.

Without looking up, she flicked her cigarette and switched hands so that her phone was to the right, arm extended straight out, unbent at the elbow. Whoever was on the line was talking to no one. Meanwhile, Caro was trying with her left hand to grab another cigarette. I put our coffees on the ground and reached into her purse. An American male voice started yelling, "Fuck you, hoe. Come back tomorrow at noon and we can sort this out. Are you there? Are you there? Are you there?"

Caro mouthed, "Be quiet," at me, and I nodded, putting the cigarette between her lips. They were half chapped, edges of dead skin around the frosted pink.

"Hang up," I mouthed to her. She shook her head.

'You're a whore, a motherfucking whore."

She was holding open the flap on her bag so I could get her lighter out.

"Hang up," I mouthed again, but the screaming had already stopped, or he had cut the line.

Defeated, Caro dropped the phone into her bag and took the lighter out of my hand. I knew better than to ask anything until she offered. She slumped down onto her haunches, elbows on knees, eyes to the sky. The street could no longer see under her long dress.

"It's okay," I said, squatting next to her while trying to hand her the coffee. She took it with her free hand, without meeting my eyes. I'd never seen her cry before. Rotten eye makeup betrayed what had happened. After two big, long swallows of coffee, she spoke, at first in a whisper. "I have to go back tomorrow."

"You don't have to do anything."

"I do, because that guy's the best friend of the singer I told you about's fiancé. He's some kind of big deal."

"Who gives a fuck?"

"I can't fuck this up for her."

"Was he a client?"

"No, I was dating him and he didn't realize what I did for work."

"That's what he was yelling about?"

"Yeah," she said and blew a smoke ring. "He said I should have told him and he's disgusted and that I'm a fraud and he's going to make sure Alex ends things with Mary and that he knows her friends are trash."

"Dude," I said it aloud, meaning "Seriously."

"Did you just call me 'Dude?'" She spit out some of her coffee and started to laugh.

"I did," I said moving out of the way.

Up until then, I had seen her only as a kind of distant acquaintance, my stand-in for "a friend." And this had been why I liked her, because I could keep her at arm's length and she didn't ask for or want more. It was enough to have coffee and cigarettes; we didn't need to share secrets.

"That made me laugh," she said, and paused. Then, very seriously, "I'd rather be Dude than Trash."

"Two things: One, anyone who calls anyone else 'trash' is a piece of shit. Two: I guarantee that guy made his money from things far worse than your honest work."

"I have to convince him not to tell Alex." Her voice was starting to rise into a sob. She took two drags to keep it down.

"What you need to do is convince your friend that she's about to marry a guy whose best friend is a bad dude."

"Margot. For real."

"For real."

"You need to stop." And then I realized she was only a stand-in. She wasn't going to go that way ever. "I need to meet him at noon tomorrow. I'm going to text him." Dropping her empty cup on the ground, she took out her phone and poked at the screen. She waited in silence, staring at it for three minutes.

Not reaching for a fresh cigarette, not moving at all. At last she announced:

"Noon at 1 West 72nd. The top." She laughed and shook her head.

"Seriously," I said, only half-question. "Gotta go to work."

On mornings when I arrived very early at the shop, I had to be alert to this one man who would sometimes turn up at almost the same moment I did, only to pace back and forth behind me as I worked the lock. I had a firm notion when I first saw him that he wasn't dangerous, not really. There was a tenderness in his gait, one that I rarely saw on uptown sidewalks, and a kind of blitheness—an attunement to my own movements. I began to bring him coffee. That was my third order from the café where I met Caro on her bad morning.

When I got to the shop, though, the man was nowhere to be seen. I brought his coffee inside with me and put it next to the colored pencils. Strange for him not to show up. I knew he was fine. His nonarrival didn't worry me, but I felt it signified a coming shift. I'd begun to see that no one was going to force me in any direction. That, plus the expectation that I'd soon find out additional life-changing news from a third party, which was becoming synonymous for online. This could mean the Internet or a rewired old-world radio, in both instances waves that were a third party in all our lives.

When you know the information itself is intended to be unreliable, you look differently at the universe's selective announcements. Privacy maintains both emotional and energetic sovereignty.

And this was very, very lonely. I understood more and more how important my parents were to each other, and their singular bond. The stakes could be pancakes and it would still hold. The problem with scaling social ladders, which was not an affair for assassins, was that as you rose the emotional bonds became more tenuous—interchangeable, even. Desire for exposure to a network could lead to corruption and the dilution of steadfast ties. Not always, but sometimes. And I feared this for Caro—this or worse. She had twenty-four hours to change her mind.

I went behind the counter and placed my purse on the shelf as usual. There was another bag there, though, which was very unusual. A woman's bag in caramel leather. Inside was a lipstick, a pack of cigarettes, a book of matches from Whitey's in Boston, and an iPhone that was turned off. It could all have been my mother's, inside and out, which put a sadness on me. I took out my own phone and wrote to her: "I'm lonely as Hell."

She and I always capitalized "Hell." A little thing that developed over the long years of our texting, and part of the extended image-language carried on between us. Like our shared Latinisms. I knew that if Iggy had seen the photos we exchanged, even with no context to color in the gaps, he, too, would have understood them as dialogue. Likewise my father. Tribes and the workings of their languages.

My mother wrote back: "That never killed anyone, it's the other way around."

"Hahaha," I wrote back. "Hell."

It was the sort of thing I would have screen-shot and sent to someone I loved, if that one person weren't already on the other end of the line.

There was a sudden sharp rap on the door. I picked my phone up off the counter and went slowly to the front of the shop. The glass panel was cracked, just like the burst in the old vanity. A dripping sound came from behind me, and I turned to see that the third coffee had spilt all over the display of colored pencils. Brown liquid began to pool on the white notepads where our few customers were encouraged to scribble and try out the merchandise. Steam rose up from the hot slop, turning colors a shade or so lighter when seen from afar. Dark red to pink. Navy blue to two shades before baby blue. And then came a certain smell. Like coffee mixed with urine. There was another sound, not a rap now but a knock. I expected to see my morning friend, but it was another male face at the door.

I first clocked that his eyes seemed gentle, disarming, but he entered by putting his fist through the glass and reaching a gloved hand right through to where the handle was. My phone hadn't yet locked itself, and I kept my finger alive on the text screen to keep it so, and pressed down to copy what was there. Without much thought I sent it to the other open window. "Hell" straight to "Tom/Card Shop." The man's feet came down hard, once then twice on the old tile floor, and then the sprinklers went off. He was far more surprised than I was to be showered, and simply walked himself out the door empty-handed and close-mouthed. The sprinklers stopped, leaving only a damp cave smell. A telephone set back on the second bottom shelf next to the register rang. I hadn't ever noticed the landline. I picked up the red plastic receiver. "Hello?"

"Are you in your head?" I laughed. It was Tom.

"I'm fine."

"I saw the whole thing on camera. Don't you worry, that one operational sprinkler doesn't reach the stationery. There's a mop in the closet next to the watercolors." He hung up.

I couldn't keep myself from laughing at this vaudeville-glamorous underworld of reverse criminals. An irreverent bloodline can set you off in all sorts of directions. No one can call which way it's going to flow. I was soaking wet. He had told me where the mop was, but not a change of clothes.

The door to the closet was painted red, age-betrayed by scales of gray and a shady halo around the metal doorknob. It was such a strange space, untouched by anything but time since the 1980s and yet somehow a fake of an original. Not unlike Disneyland in the 1950s, or the speakeasy bars everywhere in the early 2000s.

Inside the closet a single mop was leaning against the wall, underneath it what looked like a pile of green rubber on the floor. I took it out and wiped up the mess, moving it towards the front door, which remained closed, cold air coming in through the broken glass. The sprinkler hadn't been on long enough to do any real damage. I didn't feel fear or even confusion: a void. It seemed like this or something like this was set to happen after I'd seen Caro. I knew I would check on her later, tomorrow if not today. I had resolved to do so, and memorized the address in her text. This felt more significant than the morning's intruder. Caro and the absence of my friend, his coffee gone now anyway.

There was nothing to do but secure the door and clean up. It made me think of when I was approached by the modeling scout and then not long after by the old man with the address. Was my missing morning guy the real thing, or was the would-be burglar, or were both just the things-before-the-thing, signposts on the route our bloodline set for me? In biblical magic, you don't pray for the actual act, you wish for the courage and wherewithal to make it true, to conjure the kill. Before I left, I put the mop back in the closet, and then—I couldn't resist— picked up the strange rubber things on the floor. It was a pair of high boots, waders. I had admired a similar pair worn by a friend in pictures she'd sent me from a fishing trip in Montana. Weak and tired, nevertheless I decided to take them home to try on—a small delight after the wreckage of the day.

I called Caro as soon as I woke up. There was no answer, which wasn't uncommon. Her meeting was set for noon, though, and it would be unlike her not to get up early and work out. Despite being a chain smoker, she somehow believed that an expensive oversubscribed aerobics class would prepare her for whatever lay ahead.

I'd gone on dates with men akin to Caro's conquest, Alex's friend, Louis Jr., being one. The geriatric grad student didn't even come close to these characters. Nothing was ever off limits because there were no stakes. Disgustingly, financially set undue to any efforts of his own, he let his desperation for purpose play back on loop as a stand-in for bravado. The first to cast judgment on someone else's intentions, feigning purity out of false pride. How dare Caro do sex work and not tell him? Acting authoritative and victimized all at once.

I had heard all of this in the desperation of his voice yelling from her cell phone. The end of each word ascendant and echoingly hollow, having the opposite effect of what the man at the shop expressed with just his eyes. Something significant, something bred of need was missing for Alex as it was for Louis. He didn't want for much and that was the reason he was looking for a fight, seeking character in hollow confrontation.

My phone rang and I was surprised to see Caro's name. She was a big texter, a rare caller.

"What's up?"

"I'm going over there in twenty minutes."

"Has there been more communication?"

"I had to block him. He just kept going on about how I embarrassed him and how I was a whore."

"Why are you going there if you blocked him?"

"I have to make this right."

"How can you make it right? He's wrong."

"Trust me. I have to do it for her."

"Mary? She's going to be fine."

"No, remember this guy threatened to tell Alex all these things about her."

"How does he know anything about her?"

"I told him."

I couldn't answer right away. Caro had tried to bond with an unavailable suitor by sharing social secrets: ones that invalidated her best friend.

"That address he gave you is the Dakota."

"Yeah, his family owns that. He lives there when he's here."

"Where does he live when he's not here?"

"A few places."

"Yeah, that's what I thought. You're going over now?"

"Yeah."

"Please be careful."

"I'll be fine." She cut the line. I had felt the need for some kind of release since getting home from the shop last night. A run might have helped, but I also felt unable to move. Still nothing from Iggy. I had thought about asking my mother, but again came that strange sensation of mutual betrayal.

If not Iggy, who would tell me what to do, with my two gigs, Card Town clerk and International Latin Society, and beyond them? There was no need to rush things, but maybe that's what everyone says, only to look back and laugh when the years take timidity away. So I just read alone in my room, settled into the corner of the wall. This was my preferred place. No pillows, just the hard corner behind me. My phone left plugged in and far across the room. I had it set so that all calls went straight to voicemail, but I could see them registered in red as "missed."

When incoming messages showed up after the call, I was able to collect myself, get the necessary composure. No one really called anymore anyway, which was why it was so strange that Caro had done so earlier. Even Tom's call to the landline, explicable and pragmatic though it was, had jarred me. And now Caro. I got up to check on her. There were seven missed calls. "Caro" in red, and then in red a half-dozen more times. I put on the NYPD sweatshirt and ran downstairs.

When the taxi pulled up to the Dakota, I handed the driver two twenties and leaped out. I didn't bother to introduce myself at the front desk before taking the elevator to the top floor. It opened to a smell that was dank and familiar, and the penthouse door slightly ajar. No one appeared to greet or acknowledge me, but a woman dressed in an old-timey maid's uniform, the kind production companies must source from specific period wardrobe suppliers, was standing still, as though waiting, in the antechamber.

"Where did they go?"

She adjusted her white starched apron before looking at me and nodding as if she'd been waiting for someone to ask just this. "She was screaming."

"What's your name?" I asked.

"Jenny."

"Okay, Jenny. Tell me exactly what you saw."

"She was being carried out by a little man. She didn't want to go."

"What do you mean?"

"Kicking her legs, not happy. Then, the legs stopped."

"Where did they go?"

"They took the stairs. Child napping."

"There was a child asleep?"

She shook her head and motioned for me to follow. After checking over her shoulder to be certain I was alone, she used her key to open the second door that led into the apartment proper. The familiar smell was amplified here, earth and chemical both: hardcore weed with turpentine. Produced and synthetic, costly.

The nightstand in the first bedroom had been kicked over. Broken glass covered the left side of the floor. No blood, but a syrupy stain on both the carpet and the linen skirt. Jenny bent down to look under the bed and pulled out one black ankle sock and a cell phone. She handed me both. I accepted them and gently asked her again. "A child?"

"Kidnapping," she said. And I understood.

"He took her?"

"Yes. She didn't want to go with him, but they left. Down the backs stairs. She wasn't well."

"Does he have a driver?"

"I don't know."

"What else do you know about him?"

"I saw that woman smoking cigarettes outside when I first got to work."

"What about the owner of the apartment, though?"

"He's not the owner. He's the son."

"Is there a security room?" She pointed to the floor.

"Thank you. I have to go now," I said still holding the sock and phone. "Are you okay?"

"Help her."

I took the elevator down and went to the front desk to see if I could find the security office. A man in a blue suit named Mickey took me to a room under the stairs next to the freight elevator. He even didn't ask me any questions: He knew which room I needed to see, and which camera. A repeat episode, a franchise led by criminal behavior, the bloodless kind.

"This guy has a big SUV that pulls out of the back. I can tell you the license plate, but see for yourself," he said.

"Why are you so sure it's this guy?" I asked.

"Look, by law, I can't give you anything concrete, but I've seen all kinds of things. Not even what they taught me up at John Jay had me ready for what I see here. That little man walks in and it's bad news."

"Don't call the police," I said. "I have a guy, don't worry."

He nodded. "Danny from the Precinct—"

"How do you know about that?"

"Danny hangs out at one of the bars we all go to. There aren't that many cop bars left uptown. He once showed us a picture of his Lady. Couldn't of missed you if I tried." He pointed to my sweatshirt. "That's his?" I blushed and he looked down. "Maybe I shouldn't have said that." I laughed and put my hands on his shoulders, reaching up high to do so.

135

"It's okay, don't worry. That's the better of two possibilities."

He looked a little confused. "That's a balanced reaction, from a woman."

I patted him on the back. His instincts weren't wrong, only the way he communicated them and then not much. A keen feminine sense; the more balanced divinity.

"You know Danny Boy just got a promotion?" he asked, seeming pleased to have some gossip or intel to impart.

"Oh, really? We haven't spoken in a while. I was just about to text him to come meet me here."

"I'll do it. We'll surprise him." He kept nodding his head like there was an 80s rap song playing inside. "Danny Boy is on his way. He said 'Five minutes.' I've never seen him respond so fast. But then I did tell him you were here."

"Play it all before he arrives," I said. He looked confused for a moment and then realized I meant the security tape. I sat on my haunches in the swivel chair and we watched Caro being carried out. She fought back before her body went limp. I could see she'd been drugged by the continued sick flick of one ankle, like the head tick in a case of possession. It continued even when the man dropped her on the ground like firewood. I could see that it was Louis. He waved his hand and someone opened the rear passenger door. A beautiful round face showed for a second from the back. On the small screen, she was distorted into a kabuki mask: black and white with thick eyebrows. Whoever it was had been waiting for him to bring Caro down to where they were waiting in the car. There must have been a driver too—within seconds, the car sped away.

"Here he is!" Mickey said, as a cop walked through the door. At first, Danny tried to play it cool, but nodded when he saw me. I laughed a little. He didn't smile. "How's it going, man?"

"Same deal as yesterday."

"Not quite. Looks like we have something here."

"Can you play it for me?" Mickey nodded and started the tape for a third time. I had already memorized the license plate: TKMPA1.

"Danny, you don't need to write it down, I can tell you the letters. Mickey, can you zoom into that creepy face in the back?" We all watched in silence as she came into focus: the same face on the billboard over Houston Street.

"Fuck," I said.

"You know her?"

"You don't?"

"She looks like that singer Mary Cosossart."

"Yes. That's her."

"Why would she be involved in this?"

"That's the drugged woman's best friend. She's dating the best friend of the guy carrying her. I assume he's driving."

"Who's best friends with who? The little man?"

"Ha, yeah. Louis Jr."

"Who is that?"

"His family owns half of this block—maybe the whole thing."

"What do you need me for?" Danny asked.

"Can you run the plate?"

"They own the block?"

"It was an exaggeration, but a small one."

He took out his phone. "What's the second thing?" I rolled my eyes.

"I want you to protect me."

"After you broke up with me?"

Mickey looked uncomfortable. "I should go."

"Stay, it's fine. Right, Daniel?" I called him that when I was pissed.

"Don't call me that."

"Look, we have to help Caro."

"That's who that is? I thought you didn't even like her."

"Do you have your car? I know where she might be, fuck your little Fed machine. This is taking too long."

"I'm not a Fed."

"Please."

"'Please, you *are* a Fed'? Or 'Please, let's go?'" I grabbed his hand and pulled him into the hallway. "Thank you, Mickey!" I yelled as we left the building.

"Where did you park?"

"Out front."

"I bet they went to the redbrick building in Tribeca. Mary's entertainment company is in there; so is Alex's office. It's the one on West Broadway. Open my side." He obeyed and I got in the car and took out my phone. It didn't make much sense that she hadn't texted, only called so many times. It marked her own ambivalence, the desire to be kidnapped, although that seemed too aggressive a term for the crime. Louis had zero need for ransom, he only wanted control.

Danny pulled up to the front of the building. "You getting out here?" I shook my head. "No?"

"Yeah, I'm getting out here," I said.

"Then, why are you shaking your head?"

"Because you're being an idiot."

"I came to help you. I didn't have to."

"Charming. So, I go in and you stay here?"

"Yes, I am the getaway driver."

"You're in a fucking police car."

"Unmarked."

I flicked up my chin and then bent to unlock my door again. I heard him turn on the radio as I got out and walked towards the apartment building.

The doorman greeted me in a strangely familiar way, clearly mistaking me for someone else. "They are up there," he said. There was never a break-and-enter more simply executed, access cheaply gained. "Are you that actress?" he asked.

"Yes, that's me," I said without breaking stride. "Which floor again?"

"Go to seven, but it's a duplex." The fancy elevator smelled not the opposite of dirt and piss but the try-hard version. That particular perfume and the sound of a bad European beach party coming hard through the hall. I felt dizzy and nauseated. The music was loud, but I couldn't hear much human percussion: no feet at all. Someone yelled what sounded like my name, which seemed impossible. My hearing was always so sharp; perhaps it was that the smell and sounds of the staged setting were just unnerving. I took sunglasses from my purse and put them on before opening the door.

There was Caro slumped under a pastoral landscape painted in acid colors. I admit I paused for a minute to look at it closely.

It was rare for me to see a work bought on the secondary market, one that wasn't stolen.

I needed to check Caro's temperature and pulse. Her bare feet were pulled up under her, caked in dirt from God knows what or where. I picked up her left hand. It was warm, with dried blood caked right up the arm, two of her long, frosted fingernails broken off. I touched the crusted stain and realized it was actually a strange beauty mark, which I'd never noticed before. No longer in active struggle, she looked uncharacteristically peaceful below the electric country scene.

"Caro!" I said her name loudly while holding both of her hands. Nothing. "Caro." I put my hand on her chest. She was breathing slowly, then suddenly sobbing a little. "Hey, hey, Caro."

"This isn't like raising the dead in a movie." It was the same unmistakable voice that had said my name before. I turned to see a handsome man watching us from across the room.

"What?"

"You look like you're casting a spell. Very appropriate, Bath."

"How do you know my name?"

"We've met before."

"Have we?"

"I'm James."

"What are you doing here?"

"Waiting for you," he said, and then as if that was a mistake, fumbled for something else, but found nothing and said no more.

"What?"

"I knew you'd come."

"What the fuck are you doing, James?" The silhouette of a small man appeared in the doorway at the back—the same voice from that day on the phone.

"She's not well," he said.

"Leave her. She's fine." It was unclear whose side James was on—maybe a third one, which seemed more likely.

"She's not fine."

"Who are you?" Louis asked me.

"This is Bath," James said.

"Like in baseball?"

"No, but yes—kind of. Bath is friends with Caro."

"I said leave her," Louis said, ignoring James' words and me altogether.

"Look, man. She has something to do tonight, her friend is here to get her."

"Something to do tonight?" Louis repeated James' words and sneered. "Leave her, and you should go, too. We've discussed what you came here for."

James bent over and flipped Caro onto his shoulder.

"What's going on in there?" Another voice said from the kitchen.

"It's the whore's friend, Alex."

"Sorry, I can't stay very long," I said, and turned to James. "Let's go!" Neither of us spoke until we were in the elevator with Caro held between us. She started to cough a little. "You'll see an SUV on the corner with a surly, handsome man behind the wheel. I'll get in the front; you go in the back with her."

"Who's this?" Danny asked, visibly upset at James' arrival.

"James."

"James?"

I nodded. Danny was staring at him in the rearview mirror. Caro was starting to come to. She sat up, lifting her head from James' lap.

"Drive, please. Can you take us to 47 Avenue A?"

"What's there?" he asked, surely feigning some degree of ignorance.

"Just drive." Danny was visibly upset. "The point was to get Caro back and safe," I reminded him.

"I'll drop you three off there."

"Perfect," I said, and watched out the window as we turned onto Canal Street and kept going towards the Card Shop. Danny was playing second-wave grunge on the radio; Caro was crying quietly, holding her head.

I texted Tom so he would know we were coming. He was at the corner when we pulled up, ready to help James lift Caro onto the street. Danny didn't get out of the car. He was angry with me. Instead of taking the larger view or even the opportunity of our precarious moment, he saw only his competition.

Danny's craven pouting and his stubborn call of duty ended any chance of us seeing each other—on purpose—ever again. "Who is that guy?" he asked again, this time about Tom, when the three of them were indoors and out of sight. I knew I would have to explain Danny's continued presence to Tom later too. His instruction to get rid of him had been clear.

"A friend of my father's," I said.

"You've never talked about your father."

"He died."

"You've never talked about anything in your life to me."

"Danny, we are not doing this now."

"You ended things and then called when you had a use for me."

"Are you serious?"

"Completely serious."

I looked out the back window. "I have to go."

"I don't understand who any of these people are."

I got out of the car and shut the door, then bent down to the window, which he'd lowered to caution me about the bike lane. "Bye, Danny. Thank you." He started to say something else, but I walked away before he could.

There was a customer inside the shop, which was unusual. Tom had gone back to manning the register. I walked past him and into the back room where Caro was slumped at the table. Her very blue eyes were still glassy black, her chin resting in her dirty hands. James was on his phone in the corner. I saw him hang up furtively when I entered. Sitting down next to Caro, I put my hand on her back. She rudely shook it off and looked away.

"Why did you do that?" she asked.

"What do you mean?"

"Also, why do they keep calling you that other name?"

"Caro, we need to get you to a doctor."

"I'm fucking fine, and you really shouldn't meddle in other people's lives."

"You called me seven times. I heard him on the phone in the street yesterday. You were drugged—"

"I didn't ask to be rescued." I looked over my shoulder. Somehow James had found himself a porcelain mug and was drinking something slowly out of it.

"I think you need to calm down—"

"Why am I in this dump?" She got up and stumbled a little before regaining her footing. "Where are my shoes?"

"You need to relax," I said, trying to take her hands. She held them tight, close to her chest, and looked at me as if she was about to spit or vomit or both, and then broke away and walked towards the door. It took her three tries to work the handle.

I didn't see Danny again after that day, but James stayed around in one way or another for the next seven years.

"Do you want to get something to eat?" James asked. We had agreed to meet in the park uptown. It had been months since the Caro debacle, and I had done my best to keep my distance, but he had been persistent in a way I'd never encountered before, a way that made the grad student seem diffident in comparison.

After the incident, James explained that he'd been at Louis's that day because he'd arranged a meeting with Alex there about some Jiu-jitsu camp he wanted to start overseas. Turned out he was a cryptographer, a pro fighter turned cryptographer, nearly fifteen years my senior. He didn't look that old, which was strange for someone who was always out to sea. His father had been some kind of diplomat stationed in Nicaragua—in Popoyo—when he was a child. At least that was at the origin story he told me. Over time, I discounted this story, because I could tell by the way he adjusted to people that he hadn't really been raised in only one place. If you pay attention, you start to see these kinds of things. I still can't account for how he found that mug at the Card Shop.

"I could have a little something."

"Good, let's go to that sushi place you love." He tried to take my hand, but I refused.

"Not in public," I said to him quietly. Even though I didn't trust him, I liked him. He would be good to have around when I graduated in a few weeks and had hours to occupy. Someone as home base, when everything else was so uncertain. "Let's walk, okay? It's so beautiful out."

"Whatever you want."

"Can I ask you something?" I didn't wait for his answer. "Whatever became of the Jiu-jitsu camp plan?"

"I never took their calls again."

"After all that effort?"

"They are awful people."

"Yeah, neither the associates nor enemies you need, I guess." He shrugged.

"There are plenty of VC guys all over this city."

"Where's your office?"

"My office? I don't have an office, really. I do my thing out of my apartment."

"Cryptography out of your apartment?"

"You've seen too many movies. It's really very boring."

"I'd like to see your place later." He smiled.

"That is possible."

"That wasn't code," I said, also smiling.

We walked together for nearly forty blocks. By the time we got to the sushi place it was pitch black outside. I'd tried to get information out of him, but he was too clever and funny, elliptical. I told him about the Latin Research Society, and he said he knew a building that was looking for a nonprofit tenant. This seemed like a good tip, but also a way to keep tabs on me.

If there was another reason he was there that day—some agenda in his pursuit of me, I could handle that. I wouldn't allow myself to become invested in him, but the fact that he was allowing himself to fall in my direction made all the difference. His interest in me—whether as a woman or a darker thing—was at least sincere. After we ate, we went back to his place and I was able to get a look at his cryptographer's desk.

He showed up to my apartment one evening after some pick-up game, when I had just gotten out of the shower. "This is never gonna be anything else," I said, backing up towards the wall. It was strange he didn't smell like he'd been playing sports, which I should have understood to mean he hadn't. Still, my curiosity was greater than the rest. I decided to allow this, but I undressed myself.

He laughed and pulled me to him, tried to take my face in his hands. In protest, I closed my eyes and then kissed him. He tasted and smelled of fancy soap, like a wash. I was careful not to recoil, not that it would matter because he'd have taken it just as he had my earlier honest pronouncement: a challenge to be met with defiance. All I really wanted was to be clear from the start.

If James were good at his job (the hidden one) he would be seeing the contradictory signs, like me taking off my own clothes, not looking at him. There was a second explanation, though: that he saw everything. He kept kissing me. Eyes closed, I pulled away and his body still followed mine. I led us to where my back was up against the wall. I turned my face away and reached down to take off his shorts, his accession. In defiance, I threw them across the room. They hit the opposite wall and fell into a pile of mesh next to my towel. He didn't try to flip me over or to pause and shake me into telling him what was wrong. He went along for efficiency and execution. Come and be finished. It wasn't like that for me. Not with him or anyone—well, not no one. I reached behind me and put my hand on his hand that had been on my neck and then around my back. The false romance was there in his snap reaction, a replay of the arm-overhead twirl, like in the movies. He didn't realize that it was this that would allow me to turn my back to him and open my eyes. All that unspoken exchange, the actual sex wasn't worth much. Even less, from behind. Never saw it. Didn't want to. I closed my eyes again and faced the wall blindly. It would go like this for years. I knew this—us-we—was never about connection, because he allowed us to follow this playbook the first time.

His eyes however had never closed, and I had sensed them all along on my ass. Later this would cede to a hard pause, as he considered whether he could conquer me that way. It had nothing to do with violation or pain or earned intimacy, only that I would always withhold something I knew he wanted, because he was never really in.

Not that I was, either.

This dynamic kept up for some time. I tried to stave it off. He would be gone for a month somewhere and I would be happy for the absence. Too much time together spelled the end. The loose parts were what held together our entanglement, at least for me. We never discussed being in a relationship. I thought it was a given that we were not, but that may have been a generational difference. Six years later, he would say that I'd always been his girlfriend. I wasn't anyone's girlfriend.

Even when I didn't answer his calls, he would find a way back in after months of silence. I only ever went to his house; I refused him entry to the apartment I moved into in the East Village. He never met me at Card Town again, even when I started to work there four days a week after I graduated. Tom made sure I got a salary, and I made sure I was on hand for anything he needed, which meant various operations. He said I had to wait for my gun. A second graduation.

On the other days, I opened shop at the Latin Research Society, inviting school-age children to come for lessons with alumni and scholars. It was pretty successful right away; a certain kind of parent was happy to pay crazy money for their child to learn classics at a young age. I told Tom about it and he was very proud, said we were making the next generation. Of what, though?

I knew it was Caro even before she turned around. When I came in, I saw only her back behind the desk, the crisscross of laced straps fastened with a blindly tied bow. I knew it was her because of the beauty mark on the back of her left arm. The way in had also been marked with a cross, two pieces of cardboard, one vertical laid over one turned on its side, covering a structural hole. To the right of this entrance was a metal keypad. I didn't know the code, but she welcomed me through the speaker. The last of them to be resurrected?

"We were expecting you." It didn't surprise me to hear her voice, people were always reappearing in different roles. I dragged my trunk over the cobblestoned walkway that led past the stone entryway to the main building and the lobby.

She wouldn't look at me from the other side of the desk, even as she asked what I knew she would, "Are you sure you should leave it so close to the fire?"—meaning the suitcase I'd lifted onto the pale red Berber rug. When she finally turned around, I could see that she was wearing a full white Swiss-dot apron over jeans and a black long-sleeved T-shirt, sleeves rolled up. On any other given trip, I wouldn't have left my luggage close to an open flame, but she didn't know that. It was her peace offering, to forget both our pasts. I accepted with return erasure: "What's your name?" She looked me in the eye then. She had the same blue eyes.

"Frances," Caro said.

"Enchantée," I replied. "I'm Margot, but you knew that." Frances lifted her shoulders right where the white embroidery coiled into loops, both shrug and acknowledgment.

"You can have room 113."

"Cool."

"It's ready. I'll call Sam to help with your things. What's that in the basket?" She gestured at my left hand.

"It's some honey and cheese I got at the traiteur. I thought maybe I would resell it at my next stop." Frances laughed.

"For real?"

"Yes." We both after all had long known about selling things based on a cover. And the energy shifted, as it does when two people agree to honor a story. "Have you seen Mary?" I knew she had married Alex. The wedding had been talked of everywhere five years ago.

"She lives in a chateau not far from here, for half the year," Frances said, loosening the ribbon of her apron. She raised her hands to her shoulders and pulled off the arm straps. Without the apron, she looked like her doll self, younger and more vulnerable, as I remembered her, volatile, shivering instead of cool and distant. "You know Louis died? Overdose—or suicide." She broke character for a moment. "I only know this because the police contacted me to ask about him, years later, of course."

"They always come with death before they ask questions." Frances folded the apron first in half then in quarters, placed it on the desk and patted it down. I remember the last comment I'd seen online before Caro disappeared there, too. "Only Fans to Inn keeper."

That night, something fell to the floor somewhere in the house. It must have been from high because when it slammed into the ground there was a sound like none I'd ever heard before. And then smaller ones, like pieces of whatever had time to bounce beating on the concrete floor. I heard a door slam, closed. No sound of footsteps emerging. James had conveniently gone to get cigarettes. He had smoked when we first met, then quit for four years, and was at it again.

Whoever slammed the door had done so to keep something in. I would have liked to go to sleep, because there were no footsteps out of the room, but this meant someone was stuck on the other side. Motionless-still. I let go of the pillow I was holding to my chest and reached for the glasses on the nightstand, putting them on before I sat up and opened my eyes. Another hit to the floor.

The smell of smoke was rising, but I still couldn't see much. Just the dark vanity across the room, looking the same as it had when I had gone to sleep. I lifted one leg out of the bed; I was still in one piece, slight and shadow-like. It was all so black that I could barely find my way to the toilet.

And then, when I got to the real smoke, I could no longer see even the dark. I put my hands out to both sides to feel, as I'd been taught, through the room. There is a way you can sense objects and obstacles. I knew the path to the door was clear.

There was no smoke outside the room, which seemed strange after any sort of explosion. Only the smell of New York air. Cut grass, no fire. I couldn't see the stairs clearly ahead, but all the other signs of smoke were absent. I thought perhaps I was exhausted, delusional, but even in an off-planet state I was able to synthesize what I could see and feel and what was in between. Absence was easiest to identify. It's always a clean place, like when James came back over and over and Iggy hadn't come through. No crashes to the floor. Not from him or on that night. A void that remains a stand-in for lived experience. And that evening there was no smoke to fill it. Two people had already died, two kept coming back, but only one in true resurrection.

Smoke is often a gift, a fair warning to save space and suffering. Its entrails flare up to prevent the worst end. I couldn't see anything. Silence. I felt my way to the stairs and walked down, found my way to the front door and opened it to the sounds of an East Coast morning. I took off my glasses and shook my head, looked out to the tree where he'd found them both hanging. It was lit up, illuminated. Suddenly, no more fog or darkness, only the soft outline of their tree. Underneath the broken branch was one of the guy's old ATVs, a Yamaha Banshee. Someone had mentioned it in an offhand comment at dinner, unaware of its portent.

James had come home earlier than expected two nights ago to tell the house about the twin suicides. Two at once, a pact. There were things that didn't add up. Why was it James who'd found them? Why was he gone now, at the very moment of the blast? Why had he left me alone?

But then James appeared out of the fog and smiled at me. "What's funny?" I asked. He came closer, put his right arm around my shoulder, and reached for my hand with his left. I stiffened. He didn't take my hand, but instead took my glasses. "You're something else," he said, and raised them up in the air. I followed his hand and my senses, all of them, realigned at what he'd shown me. "Why were you wearing sunglasses?" I laughed. And then what he said changed everything. "We need to talk about what happened at the house."

"Where were you?"

"No, I mean when you were fifteen."

I decided to go back to the city alone after that morning. James acted like he had a sense of something traumatic having happened to me, but I knew he had been told by someone else and any sense he had was secondhand or slighter. I had never really trusted him. There had been a neat disconnect because I trafficked in an ancient language and he in code. Nothing, ever, was one to one. This allowed the connection a plasticity but kept it from getting all that deep. With Iggy, it was the reverse: we hadn't spoken in years, but what was between us still held weight—for me. It was alive, but suspended in 4D.

I think it is because of my mother's sea-nymph rescue—an inborn original sin—that my wires were forever crossed. An aborted suicide attempt that gave life to not one but two people. Again, if anyone can say they tried to get out of it, I can. I didn't fear my own disappearance, because of that connection. I had no fear except the fear of finding someone I truly couldn't lose, which I believed was Iggy, and not Iggy because he was already gone.

Unable to sleep the evening after I returned to my apartment, I asked Alyssa if she'd meet me in Washington Square Park late at night. She took the last train to the city.

"Bath," she called me from the bench beside the jungle gym where someone had painted the railing dark blue, scaling in places, like the door handle of the closet where I'd found the waders. Outside at night, these flakes exposed old skins, green in the moonlight. My body felt like this, after what had happened, another betrayal. It was as if there would always be a poison-drug in my every vein. There would be no getting rid of it, no transfusion, no magical spell. This was what would always be true. The difference between noir and cyberpunk is that red still runs through you.

Alyssa put her hand down on the empty part of the bench. I sat next to her, our heels in the playground sand.

"I never really wanted James. He only ever got in, because Iggy didn't show up."

"Have you asked him to?"

"Who? Iggy?"

"Yeah."

"No, never. If he wanted to he would."

"Bath, you're impossible. You approach love unlike anything else in your life."

"What do you mean?"

"Everything else you run towards, headfirst."

"He knows where I am."

"Does he?"

"I don't know."

"You can find out."

"That's not so easy."

"What kind of nonsense is that?"

"Old family stuff."

"You have to let that go. What about James?"

"I just don't care. There's something not quite right. And he talks a lot about purity, a protest that is always a tell."

"What does that even mean?"

"His denial is evidence of the very thing he is sounding against: a reveal, an admission."

"That's also a case against Iggy."

"Is it? He never claimed to be better than anyone or even a good guy."

"Which is why even the lesser connections shouldn't be thrown away."

"What do you mean?"

"You can't be so extreme all the time. I don't understand where this sense of warped justice comes from. People say, 'Do what you're comfortable with,' but discomfort is your thing? You barely know Iggy."

"That's wrong. You die in a single shot. You can love like that too. It doesn't mean it will work out or that you can carry on. I know the systems aren't synced like that."

"That's really sad."

"Not really." A rat ran by and ducked into the greenery behind the gate.

"Gross," Alyssa said. "It must be midnight by now."

"Yeah, we should go. Will you sleep at my place? I feel really uneasy."

"Yeah, of course."

We arrived back at the apartment to a scene like that day my parents and I got home from France and the raccoon was on the counter. Someone had broken in, and even though I had barely any possessions, had managed to make it look like they'd had both a difficult and fun time not finding whatever they'd been looking for.

"You need to call the police," Alyssa said.

"I definitely do not trust the police."

"Bath, come on. Call Danny or James."

"Absolutely not."

"You sound like a lunatic, truly."

"Look, you don't have to stay with me. I will be fine."

"I'm staying, but I'm also calling James. He can send someone over."

"He's not trustworthy."

"Honestly, Bath, I'm tired of your paranoia."

"You don't understand."

"I've known you since you were in grade school."

It really wasn't worth arguing with her. She was steadfast and still I hadn't told her all of the important things. "I'll call him," I said.

"Thank you."

The next day, James came by as soon as his plane landed. I owed it to him to have a conversation about my departure, which, of course, led to us sleeping together again. It was easier than having to confront what he had shown me. He didn't bring up the other night, so I decided to forget he knew. At the very least, I was able to operate in the world with him. Why not for a little longer? I had no one else.

My mother had been strangely quiet lately, responsive if I reached out, but otherwise gone. She didn't answer every text—only one in three, which had never happened before. No news of her, my father, or Iggy. It was only a matter of time before Tom would likely bring one of the three up. I didn't initiate the conversation. No questions meant there would be no answers on account of my own pursuit. The rules of detachment are very simple.

"I'm proud of you," Alyssa said when I met her again a week later at the park.

"Why? I'm betraying myself now."

"You can't be this beautiful hermit forever."

"I can."

"But you're not and you're outside with me."

"For now."

Later that day, my phone went off. It was Iggy.

"Can you meet me in Boston tomorrow?"

"Are you insane?"

"Why not?"

"You can't just text me out of nowhere after so long."

"Yes, but there's so much history."

"There was more once."

I stared at my phone for nearly an hour after the messages arrived. I sent a screenshot to Alyssa to be sure it was real. There it was, logged. An image saved and saved again. Resurrection this round in real time.

And then James called, interrupting my screen vigil. I answered quickly. "Hi, I might lose you, I'm going underground."

"Haha," he said.

"No, really. I have to get on the subway," I lied, and hung up.

The Latin Research Society had been overdue for a seminar in Boston. It was the first time Iggy and I spent a week together. A week that felt like three hours, full speed and also the length of a screened Hollywood romance, a classic one. It was all that: opening credits; opening night in a place neither of us had ever been, being watched.

Don't hold too many intimacies at once; that's how you keep yourself free.

I had been with James, tried to be really with him for nearly five years. We had met because of Caro, seven years ago. It became clear she had only been a catalyst, and for more than James. He had been told to keep an eye on me. I became sure of this, which didn't negate his pursuit of love and truth—that would be a wrongheaded assumption in our worlds—but his version wasn't the same as mine.

I was born an extremist and I'd die one. No one's attention should come from someone else's orders.

But after Boston, Iggy disappeared again. So, I went back.

"Bathory! What are you doing in there?" he yelled at me through the bathroom door.

"I'm in the tub, James. Please leave me alone. I will be out in five minutes." He usually called me just Bath, but something was wrong. James was always simply James, and that was part of the reason I thought I could stand to lose him.

"Bath, we are going to be late."

"It's fine. No one is ever on time to dinner." I pulled the plug out of the drain, holding up the beaded wire that connected it to the faucet. The hotel had all old appliances, including a gas stove in the kitchen and some sort of unhappy radiator. One of the night porters had told me they used to house the actors for movies being shot on and around the nearby cliffs and oceanscapes. It was cheap to shoot there—tax breaks from the government. Which government, I always wanted to ask, but they didn't know the things I knew.

And so the hotel was a kind of Hollywood hostel, which made sense because of the performative ghosts. James had insisted on taking me away from the wired city after the break-in, after I came back from the seminar in Boston. But we had just been away where bad things had happened, so he insisted that we have a redo, this time somewhere with bad service close to the sea. He also wanted to surf with his friend Ludwig.

"Dinner's only downstairs," I said through the door.

"I told Ludwig that I would go through his photos from Cairo."

"Why at dinner?" I opened the door naked, wrapping the towel around my head.

"He said he had to go fishing afterward."

"Fishing?"

"Yes, with those elaborate flies he makes. Said something about the moon tonight. And that nymphs are born in this water."

"Only you would have a friend that goes deep-sea fly fishing." I walked past him into the communal hallway before turning into the bedroom.

"You should cover up," he said.

"Everyone's at dinner." He turned around and looked at me. I picked up one of his T-shirts that he'd left on the edge of the bed and turned it inside out. He coughed. I held the shirt to the light that was still coming from the north window. The faint outline of its logo showed through on the navy-blue cloth. I preferred my father's black metal ones, but they were all in the wash when I was told I had to pack to leave the next day.
I took the towel off my hair, shook it loose, and pulled the T-shirt over my head, leaving the wet ends under its collar.

"You need to wear something practical. We will go out after to explore. It will be wet and dark."

"Always committed to finding something." He turned, coughed, and walked out. I found my jeans next to the bed, but my belt was missing. It was darker than before, the sun had gone down quickly. I put on the bottom of a white two-piece bathing suit and pulled my pants on. The bow-tied sides of the suit bottom held the baggy jeans in place for the moment. There was a row of shoes lined up against the wall, mostly hiking-style boots or sneakers. I put on a pair of flat sandals and left, pulling my hair out of the back of the shirt as I ran down the stairs. Reverse halo.

"Have you read *The Golden Ass*?" I asked James, to try and diffuse his anger. "We are reading it to the second-graders at the Foundation. It was a big topic in Boston." He was facing the water, backlit by the moon, feet unsteady at rock's edge. I knew he didn't hear me.

"James?"

He didn't turn around. There was still unwashed dirt around his ankles, visible because of the shallow glow off the water, his body otherwise blacked out against the horizon. "James!" I walked slowly towards him, over the rocks shellacked with the entrails of sea plants. Seaweed, because it's always wet, is never called foliage. There is no sound when you step on it.

Flotsam rises; leaves fall. "James?"

"You sound like you're about to say something important?" He said it deadpan, unmoved, even as I slid closer.

"Is that why you won't answer?"

"Perhaps you should have stayed in the bath, instead of embarrassing me like that."

"It wasn't intentional."

"You never have a plan."

"I do have a plan." I touched his back; his whole body registered it, but he didn't turn around.

"It doesn't involve me." It was the first time he'd ever questioned my intentions. Something had shifted and I couldn't tell if it was me or an outside plan.

"What if what I say next is the thing before the thing that changes your life?" I said.

"Set me free."

"How did you know?"

"It was a joke, what do you mean?" Over the years, he'd often done this: shook his head trying to clear away the madness of what I'd said or not said. It had always been in jest, as if he were acting in a play.

"What?" I put one arm around his waist and the other over his shoulder. He tried to sidestep it. I held on tightly.

"I don't really understand you," he said, and this time he was serious.

I stood up on my toes. "Isn't that supposed to be my line?" My hair was held in a slick, high ponytail. If I had to worry about my trousers falling, I couldn't be bothered to deal with my wet hair. I had purposely worn the wrong shoes. The bottoms were smooth, precarious. James stared at my feet. "I know what you're thinking: wrong choice of shoes."

"I wasn't thinking that. I know you chase precarity."

"What the fuck does that mean?"

"You know exactly what it means."

"I'm lost."

"Your desired destination." He didn't come closer. "Except maybe Boston." He could move more easily across the rocks, but he stood still. "What are we going to do then?"

"What do you mean?" I asked. The moon had turned sleepy,

a leathery cloud—hood—coming down into its light. All of the rocks seemed to be lit up white-blue from below. "Did you know there are nine species of deep-sea corals that can make their own light?"

"What are we going to do, then?"

"After what?"

"I mean now." He looked at me hard. "After what you said."

"Oh. I don't know, go where we both need to?" His face registered real despair.

"Don't look so upset. Stop that. Oh, fuck off. You didn't want to really be together forever anyway. I have to go."

"I did. I do." He refused to turn, remained on edge.

"I can't stay."

"You said that when I first met you. Actually, it was, 'I can't stay very long.'"

"Yes, seven years isn't very long."

I was alone again, truly alone. James was really gone, after that last trip. We both knew we'd never see each other again. What had started as a conquest, both of sex and information, had become something else to him. It was the right thing to do, to let him go. And because of our twisted bond, I knew he would never hurt me with what he knew. And Tom would take care of that if it ever became an issue.

And Iggy was gone. I'd spent days, then months, trying to figure out what I'd done wrong. When had he decided I wasn't right? And I didn't even believe in that sort of thing. I didn't want to be known, but Iggy had been right when he mistakenly said he knew me after that first New York night. But this last disappearance felt worse than all the others, perhaps because of the intensity of what had come just before. You don't fuck on a rooftop in a part of town where you can get shot and not feel anything.

Then I was back in New York again and every phone was going off with the threat of inclement weather, talking about some barometric glitch, predicting overflow of biblical proportions and apocryphal rainclouds. That bleating of caution and high alert seemed heavy-handed, as there hadn't been flooding in the Tristate area in over a decade. All of which reminded me of listening to the shipping forecast in the car over the years, passenger side.

I had to send out an email that Latin classes were suspended due to the flood warnings. Schools and businesses were closing. The lightning had started around 2 a.m. and by 5 a.m. there was thunder and a full downpour. Twelve hours of rain gave way to hail. For two hours, ice fell, then changed back to temperate rain. I decided to walk from my apartment to check on the shop. Less a decision than a compulsion.

My windbreaker would be warm enough with a heavy Irish sweater underneath. I'd grow hot on the long walk. It took a moment before I remembered the fishing boots I'd brought home from the shop so many years ago. At first, I thought they were in the front closet, but no luck. I finally found them rolled up under the laundry room sink. When I shook them out, I noticed "Peter," written in black marker upside down inside the left leg.

The streets were empty, which was something to see before the water started to really rise. It was dirty and ankle-deep by the time I got to Fourth Street and Avenue A. I could see the flower shop boarded up with wooden planks. The red light of a passing police car caught in the brown crest slapping at the front of Card Town. Something was strange about the angle of the splash; then I saw the metal shutter had been lowered over the entrance. I hadn't even realized one was hidden up in the building.

"Bath," Tom had appeared behind me in the street. "What are you doing here?" he asked, staring at my legs knee-high in water.

"I didn't expect to see you."

"Where did you get those?" he asked in a half-accusatory way, still focused on my feet.

"I'm sorry, I know I should have asked. I took them from the closet ages ago. They were yours?"

"Our brother's."

"Our?" He shook his head and waved his hand as he had so many times before in dismissal of a forbidden question. I didn't press. The sound of splashes from somewhere across the street caused both of us to turn around. A man was trying to lift off one of the boards covering the racks where the cut flowers were displayed each day. He turned to look at us before bolting. Gentle Eyes, soaking wet and once again fleeing the scene. I saw something flash across Tom's face and then disappear as he noticed the graffiti on his own storefront.

"Holy shit, I've never taken the gate down before. That must have been there a while."

"Scio te mihi futurum esse," was painted in large, dirt-caked yellow letters on the newly lowered steel door. The message had been there for me to see, if circumstances aligned, for some time.

"What does it mean?" he asked aloud, not expecting a response.

In the adrenaline of the scene, I only half answered, "I know you—" before he cut me off.

"By the way, Iggy came by." Tom said what I already knew. "He helped me close up one day. And he left a note for you, said to deliver it come hell or high water."

"He didn't say that."

"No, he didn't, but it made you laugh." I nodded as he handed me a piece of paper folded in half.

"He couldn't be bothered to find an envelope at the stationery store." Tom smiled. "Bath, I have to tell you. He's not coming back."

"I know," I said.

It started to rain again and the water began to rise. Neither of us was really bothered. We'd both seen worse. I hugged him and then watched him walk towards Third Street and turn the corner.

I stood there alone for a moment before opening the note. No date or sign-off. Only a single sentence:

"Will always said he'd raise a storm."